THE THUG
THAT SECURED
Her Heart

2

A NOVEL BY

MISS JENESEQUA

Royalty Publishing House is now accepting manuscripts from aspiring or experienced urban romance authors!

WHAT MAY PLACE YOU ABOVE THE REST:

Heroes who are the ultimate book bae: strong-willed, maybe a little rough around the edges but willing to risk it all for the woman he loves.

Heroines who are the ultimate match: the girl next door type, not perfect - has her faults but is still a decent person. One who is willing to risk it all for the man she loves.

The rest is up to you! Just be creative, think out of the box, keep it sexy and intriguing!

If you'd like to join the Royal family, send us the first 15K words (60 pages) of your completed manuscript to submissions@royaltypublishing-house.com

Synopsis

After almost losing his life at the hands of his psycho ex-girlfriend and overhearing his younger brother's possible involvement in his attempted murder, Kalmon feels like he can trust no one. Not his family, not Azia Price and not even himself. But just when he starts to warm up to everyone again, another tragedy strikes and Kalmon's heart freezes into a cold ice box. He isolates himself from everyone including the woman he's fallen deeply for. But isolating himself from her is potentially about to be the biggest mistake of his life. Especially when it quickly leads to her finding comfort in the arms of someone else. Will Kalmon no longer be able to secure Azia's heart?

For Azia, meeting Kalmon Howard was unexpected at first but turned out to be the sweetest taboo. What seemed like a new opportunity to grow with the dangerous yet charming man she's falling helplessly in love with, soon turns out to be the exact opposite once Kalmon starts pushing her away. When a friendly face makes it known that he's here for Azia in any way possible, she decides to take him up on his offer and lets him into her life, pushing her feelings for the real man she wants to the side. But will she push them away completely and ultimately push Kalmon out of her life for good?

Alongside their strained relationship, Kalmon and Azia are both unaware of the brewing conflict between those closest to them. But the brewing conflict is the least of their problems because of the secretive plots set out against Kalmon's empire. Will Azia and Kalmon be able to overcome their hardships together, or is this the abrupt and destructive end of their newly formed bond?

"So tell me how am I ever gonna find love in you
If I do not even know what I want from you
'Cause we both want different things
Why can't this be one common thing?"
—*Jorja Smith*♫

Prologue

"Y ou're going to pay for what you've done."

Her words had him confused and just as he turned around to face her, he saw the gun she was holding in her right hand. The gun didn't faze him; what fazed him was what she said.

"And what exactly have I don—"

Bang!

The gun went off and the bullet shot straight into his flesh, sending him straight to the floor.

"Ending us," she said. "That's what you're paying for, Kalmon."

Bang!

Then the next bullet came, entering him from the side. He tried to scream out but when he opened his mouth all that emerged was blood. If someone had told him months ago that this was how his life would end, he would have told them that they were nothing but a liar.

His vision was becoming blurry and he could feel his heart rate slowing down. His body was beginning to viciously shake and his entire body felt like it was on fire. He tried to lift his head up, but the intense pain radiating all over his body meant he failed. He couldn't bring himself to do anything but remain where he was, defenseless on the floor and dying.

Then the next words he heard from her made him question everything about the one man he thought he could trust in this life.

"I know you're sick of me calling you but I'm leaving you this voicemail to let you know I've killed your brother, Keon. Are you happy now? This is what you wanted, right?"

Then the darkness successfully pulled him in and he was out like a light.

Chapter One

He was making her feel good. That was undeniable. He was touching her in ways that she had forgotten she could be touched in. Providing her with that euphoria that she had been deprived of for months now. The euphoria she had convinced herself that she no longer needed. A euphoria too sweet and one that made her never want to stop what they were doing right now. The way their bodies were connecting as one soul. The way he was pushing his shaft deep within her and pulling out, only to dive right back in to keep giving her the euphoria she had been starving for. However, it didn't matter how good this all felt right now because the reality of the matter was, Iman knew it was wrong.

"Keon… wait, we… we need to stop."

Keon stopped moving and lifted his head from the corner of her neck, no longer planting seductive kisses on her flesh.

"What?"

The scrunched up expression he currently had on his handsome face told Iman of his confusion. And as much as this moment was being enjoyed by the both of them, Iman knew that it needed to come to an end.

"This is wrong."

Keon continued to look down at her with that same confused expression.

The guilt cradled within her eyes was undeniable. Instead of saying anything more, Keon gently eased out of her and stepped away.

He was frustrated at the fact that he had to slide out her heavenly slit that he had grown to love so much in the last few minutes. He was also frustrated at the fact that neither of them had climaxed yet, more her than him, but it was what it was. He wasn't about to force her to do something that she clearly had doubts about.

It was wrong of me to even make a move on her knowing damn well she's Athena's sister. It doesn't matter how attracted I am to her or how angry I am with Athena. She's fuckin' right; this is wrong.

"You right," he said in agreement before pulling up his black Calvin Klein boxers followed by his jeans. "I never should have came onto yo—"

"Oh shit, no!"

Keon blinked rapidly at Iman's sudden outburst and the way her eyes had grown large with fright. She was no longer staring at him but rather at something behind him.

When Keon turned around to spot the mounted plasma screen that showcased security cameras of Iman's bakery, his heart almost went into shock once he noticed the woman walking into the shop, holding hands with a young boy that favored him.

"Shit," Keon cursed, frozen in his stance until he felt a piece of clothing land on his face.

"Get dressed!" Iman exclaimed after throwing his shirt at him.

She quickly jumped off her desk and began putting on her panties followed by her bra. While she attempted to get clothed, her eyes never broke away from her plasma screen. When she noticed that Athena and Athan were still walking through the bakery and seemed to be walking away from the main checkout area, Iman's greatest nightmare was revealed. They were heading to her office.

What she really wanted to do was fall down and be swallowed up by the ground so that she didn't have to face the predicament that she was in right now. However, that was the very last thing she could do. The only thing she could do was somehow get out this horrible situation that she'd never imagined in a million years she could be in. Grabbing her t-shirt and jeans, Iman ran towards her office door and slid her door latch into place.

* * *

ATHENA WALKED up to her sister's office door with a smile on her face. She was actually glad to be seeing her sister. It had only been a couple of days since they had laid eyes on each other last, but Athena was excited to see her big sister regardless. That was her blood and all she had in New York city since both their parents had passed in a car accident when Athena was just ten and Iman thirteen. They had been raised by their grandmother and grandfather from their father's side.

With her right hand still holding on to Athan's hand, Athena used her free hand to gently knock on the oak door but instead of waiting for her sister to respond and grant her entry, Athena turned the golden knob to get inside. Unfortunately, the door wouldn't open.

Knock! Knock!

"Iman? You there?"

There was brief silence for a few seconds before Athena suddenly heard her sister's gentle voice.

"Just a minute, sis!"

More silence followed before Athena heard the door being unlatched and the door was finally opened. Athena tried to step forward so she could enter but Iman stepped out before she could, blocking her entry and quickly embracing her.

"Hey sis!"

At first, Athena was baffled by her sister's overly enthusiastic mood but nonetheless, she returned her sister's embrace, letting go of Athan's hand so she could wrap her arms around her sister.

"Hey, you okay?"

"Yeah, I'm good," Iman replied with a soft sigh as she held onto her sister and shut her eyes.

"I tried calling but you didn't pick up," Athena explained.

"Oh, my phone's on silent and somewhere deep in my bag."

Iman felt her heart warm a little at the truthful words she had just uttered but sadly, she knew everything else to follow in their conversation had a strong potential to be nothing but lies.

The sisters were both so caught up in their embrace and greeting one another to take strong notice of the curious eyes of the little boy in their presence. The little boy who ran straight past his mother and auntie to push wider the door that shielded Iman's office ahead.

"Daddy!"

It wasn't until she felt quick movement near her and heard him call out to his father that Iman wanted to shoot herself. Athena broke out of their embrace and looked ahead into the open office to see her man leaning on the edge of Iman's desk and their son happily running up to him.

"What's up, son?"

Keon crouched down with open arms and lovingly embraced his son, kissing his forehead before hugging him tighter. Seeing her man, made Athena's heart skip a beat and she broke out of hugging Iman so she could go greet him.

"Key... baby, what are you doing here?" Athena queried, grinning at him and walking deeper into Iman's office.

When he didn't return her grin, Athena stopped walking and felt uneasiness crawl up her spine. All he shot her was a cold look. A cold look that he hadn't given her in years.

Seeing that Keon wasn't answering her sister made Iman decide to intervene by stating, "He came to pick up cupcakes for you, Athena. Like he always does."

"Oh." Athena never took her eyes off Keon, even as Iman explained why he was here.

When he got up from hugging Athan and lifted him up to hold him against his chest, Athena stayed watching him. Without a doubt, she could see that something was wrong. His cold look had not only told her that but his silence too. Keon wasn't a silent man, especially not around her. Not only was something wrong but Iman seemed nervous, and that was enough to make Athena further suspicious. Something was off and she intended to find out exactly what.

"But why was your office door locked?" Athena asked, breaking her eyes away from her man to look at her sister.

"Oh I do that out of habit someti—"

"I locked it," Keon spoke up, cutting off Iman.

Athena's eyes darted back over to Keon. Keon, who stood tall and mighty while holding his son. He had on a short-sleeved Kenzo t-shirt and denim jeans. She hadn't seen him get dressed this morning but now that she was looking at him, heat quickly flowed between her thighs. This man was too fine to be true sometimes... more like all the time.

"Because I wanted to talk to your sister in private about why she was treating me like a bitc..." Keon's words trailed off as he looked over at Athan who was innocently observing him. He caressed his son's soft cheek before continuing to speak. "Treating me like I was nothing at the casino night, and I found out exactly what I needed to."

Oh God no... he knows.

Athena could feel her heart racing and her entire body had gotten hot.

She didn't need to look over at her sister to see the guilt written across her face. It was just something she could sense. Call it sisterly instinct.

"Keon, I swear I can expla—"

"There's nothing for you to explain," he retorted with a frown. "We're done."

"Key, please don—"

Real hot girl shit
Yeah, I'm in my bag but I'm in his too
And that's why every time you see me, I got some new shoes

This was honestly the most inappropriate time for her phone to be ringing but here it was, doing exactly that. *For Christ's sake. Any other time but now,* Athena mused before quickly pulling out her phone to silence it. Until she saw the caller ID that read Keon's mother.

It was an odd sight because Keon's mother rarely called her out of the blue. If she wanted to see her grandson, Keon made sure that she could see him whenever she wanted. Even though Athena's initial plan was to silence her phone so that she could focus on somehow saving the relationship that she thought she still had, she wanted to know the reason why Athan's grandmother was calling. Was something wrong with her?

"Nolita? Is everything okay?" Athena began to talk to Nolita, purposely avoiding Keon's intense eyes. "He's… I'm with him right now… Okay, I will."

Athena then looked over at Keon and began sauntering over to him before nervously handing him her iPhone.

"Your mother needs to talk to you."

Keon stared hard at the phone then reached for it. One hand held Athan against his body while the other now held Athena's phone to his ear. He didn't get why his mother was calling Athena, but he knew he was surely about to find out.

"Key! Everyone's been trying to get through to you," his mother fumed down the phone. "Why the hell are you not picking up your damn phone?"

"My bad, Ma. I switched it off," he said, remembering what he had done earlier. "Why? What's going on?"

"Kalmon's been shot."

Chapter Two

Twenty-nine years of being on this earth and Kalmon had never been shot before. Until this very day. His initial belief had been that he was going to die but when he regained consciousness from the bullets that his crazy ex-girlfriend had inflicted on him, Kalmon knew right then and there that God was giving him an olive branch. An olive branch he needed to climb so high and beyond.

Regaining consciousness and seeing that he was in a hospital room, all alone, also made him realize that the only person who truly had his back in this life was himself. His initial belief was that he was all alone until a woman stepped into the room.

"Kally!"

A woman that he recognized to be his mother rushed over to where Kalmon lay stretched out on a hospital bed.

"Thank God you're awake! My baby boy!"

She immediately kissed him, planting kisses all over his face and beginning to cry tears of joy.

"Ma, ease up," Kalmon spoke up with a hoarse voice, coughing slightly.

"I thought I lost you," she commented, caressing his face while looking down at him.

Kalmon gave her a blank stare before his eyes drifted over to tall figures that had now entered the room.

"Son, glad to see you awake," his father Fontaine announced with a proud smile.

"You scared us for a minute, Kal," Jahmai spoke up.

"Seriously, you did bro."

Kalmon felt his blood begin to boil as he spotted his so-called brother. The fact he had just called him bro when he was clearly anything but that had Kalmon wanting to beat the shit out of him. Or better yet kill him. One thing that Kalmon couldn't stand was betrayal, and his brother was the biggest betrayer of them all.

"Get out," Kalmon said directly to Keon, making everyone throw baffled gazes his way.

"Huh?" Keon queried.

"You heard what the fuck I just said!" Kalmon bellowed, lifting his back off his bed and clenching his fists. "Get the fuck out!"

"Kal, that is no way to talk to your bro—"

"He's no brother of mine," Kalmon interrupted his mother with a sneer. "He plotted with that stupid bitch to kill me and best believe I'm going to kill the both of you once I get out of here."

"I plotted with who?" Keon questioned his brother, not understanding what the hell he was talking about.

"Jahana's the one who fuckin' shot me," Kalmon voiced. "Because you told her to, didn't you? You just couldn't bring yourself to do it and you want me out of the way so damn bad so you can make decisions by yourself."

"I never told Jahana shit!" Keon yelled, getting pissed that Kalmon was accusing him of such a thing. "Why would I want my own brother dead? What sense does that fuckin' make, nigga?"

11

"Boys, please. Calm down," their mother pleaded with them. "And enough with all the cursing."

"Nah, fuck that! He's accusing me of trying to murder him! Are any of you hearing the bullshit that's coming out of his mouth right now?" Keon questioned his family in disbelief.

"We were told Jahana was the one who called the emergency services for you, Kal," Jahmai piped up. "You were found in her apartment alone but she was nowhere to be found…"

"Before she let me for dead, Jahana called his dumb ass and left a voicemail," Kalmon responded as he pointed directly at Keon, not caring about the new information he'd learned about Jahana calling 911. She was still to blame for the fact that he was bedridden right now. "I heard her say how she had done what you wanted and asked you if you were happy. So stop tryna lie about this shit when I've caught your ass red handed."

"I ain't heard no damn voicema—" Keon's words abruptly stopped once he came to a great realization.

"Cat got your tongue?" Kalmon spoke up, noticing his brother's new-found silence. "Or the truth got your tongue should I say instead?"

"I ain't heard no damn voicemail because I switched off my phone," Keon continued, throwing a heated stare down Kalmon's way.

For someone who was attached to a lot of wired machines and supposed to be recovering from gunshot wounds, Kalmon sure had a lot of negative energy right now. And Keon hated that it was all being directed his way.

"But Jahana called me a couple times after the casino night," Keon explained wholeheartedly. "Begging me to help me get you guys back together. But when I told her to get over you and move on, she threatened to kill you but I thought that was just her crazy ass saying shit. I didn't think she was actually going to go through with it."

"But your dumb ass still didn't say anything," Kalmon reminded him. "Now look where the fuck I am."

"Nigga, how was I supposed to know she was actually going to carry out that shit? I'm telling you the truth and here you are being a bitch despite the fact that it's your ass strapped up to those machines right now, not me."

"There's two sides to every story. But fuck your weak ass side 'cause you ain't nothing but a mothafuckin' liar."

"Nigga, I swear to God you are so lucky you're strapped to those machines right now, 'cause I'll beat the shi—"

"That's enough you two," Fontaine intervened, no longer wanting the back and forth between his sons to continue.

Kalmon refused to let it go though, because not only was he in pain right now but he was also in pain at the thought of being betrayed by his only brother. His brother who now meant nothing to him.

"I don't want anything to do with you any—"

"Enough!"

Fontaine's shout was enough to silence Kalmon and Keon from speaking any further to one another.

"Both of you need to relax. This is clearly just one big misunderstanding that will be sorted out once Kalmon is better and out of here. Let's just focus on making sure you recover speedily, Kalmon. No more arguing. Both of you just shut the fuck up and calm the fuck down."

Despite the fact that he could hear what his father was saying, Kalmon was doing anything but listening. He was still sure that his brother was plotting against him and whether he cared to admit it or not, Kalmon really didn't trust him right now. He didn't trust anyone. His only goal was to recover and get the hell out of this hospital. He hated hospitals almost as much as he hated Jahana. For what she'd done to him, she needed to die a painful and slow death. And Kalmon was more than willing to make sure that she was provided with one.

Chapter Three

B*aby, you coming 'round tonight?*
Send.

It's been a few days since I've heard from you… I hope you're okay.

Send.

I miss you… and him too.

Send.

Let me know if you're coming to see me tonight.

Send.

Azia sighed softly as she looked down at her phone screen, taking one last look at the message she had just sent to Kalmon including the previous ones she'd sent during the day. Then she locked off her phone and placed it to the side so that she could focus on burying herself in some work.

It was evening and even though she had arrived back home from work, here she was finishing off a project that she didn't need to hand in till next week. She'd already showered and fixed herself something to eat, but her work had called her. So now she found herself burying herself in it. But even as she did work, there was only one man on her mind.

He had left her three days ago with a mind-blowing love session and passionate kisses. And now more than ever, she missed him. Azia smiled at the fact that she was thinking about him nonstop. *I guess that's what happens when you're in love Zi...*

Ding!

She immediately reached for her phone, thinking that he had responded to her last text message. Only to be proved wrong when she saw her incoming notification.

Drinks one day?

Just as friends of course.

Nahmir.

Instead of responding back, Azia locked her phone and chucked it to the side. Saddened by the fact that Kalmon hadn't messaged her back yet, she decided to respond back to Nahmir minutes later.

Sure, I don't see why not.

Azia.

But still, within her creeped the desire to know if Kalmon was coming over tonight. *Let me just call him.*

Seconds later, Azia's phone was glued to her right ear, listening to the dial tone as she waited for him to pick up. The phone was eventually picked up after a couple rings and just as she was about to greet him, a familiar female voice came on the line.

"Azia?"

Oh shit. Azia felt her heart drop once realizing that Kalmon's mother had picked up the phone.

"Hi, Mrs. Howard," she awkwardly answered.

"Hi to you too, Azia," Nolita greeted her in a neutral tone. "I see your number's saved in my son's phone. Is there something you'd like to tell me?"

Yes... I'm falling for your son and having sex with him almost every night.

"Oh... well, Kalmon and I... are seeing each other."

"Uh-huh, I thought so," Nolita voiced knowingly.

"You know?"

"Of course I know, darling. Did you really think pretending to hate each other at the office was going to fool me?" Nolita let out a light chuckle. "Oh I know everything, love."

"I'm so sorry, Mrs. Howard, I didn't mean to start a relationship with your so—"

"Why are you apologizing?" Nolita asked her. "You have nothing to be sorry for."

Azia tucked her hair behind her ear and rested back against her sofa, relief filling her veins at Nolita's understanding state.

"I just wish you came into his life sooner."

"So you're okay with us being together?"

"Yeah, why wouldn't I be? You're good together. I know that every time I see you two together, because despite how much you guys love to put on a show of hating one another, you come up with great ideas together."

Azia grinned at Nolita's revelation before saying, "Thank you, Mrs. Howard."

"No need to thank me, love. And feel free to call me Nolita."

"Okay, Nolita."

"Well Azia, I hate to be the bearer of bad news but Kalmon's not coming to see you tonight."

Azia blushed at the fact that Nolita had seen her text message about wanting Kalmon to let her know if he was coming over to see her tonight. And the other text messages that Azia had sent to him about missing him and his...

"He's been in the hospital for a few days now and is probably going to be here for a few weeks."

Azia felt a sharp pain enter her chest at Nolita's mention of Kalmon being in hospital.

"Oh my gosh... is he okay?"

"He's fine now, but he was shot so he's in recovery mode. The doctors managed to get the bullets out so he's just resting."

"Oh my God!"

Azia couldn't believe it. It was now making sense as to why he hadn't answered any of her texts, calls or been at work. Nolita Howard hadn't shown up to Howard Enterprises either.

"Don't worry, love. He's in a much better state now, like I said. Why don't you take the day off tomorrow and come and see him? I'm sure he'll love that. It'll be a lovely surprise for him."

"Yes please, I'll be there for sure."

More now than ever, Azia wanted to see his face and see with her own eyes that he was really okay. She also wanted him to know that she was there for him undoubtedly.

~ The Next Morning ~

Azia had struggled to sleep properly all night. The only thing that had managed to ease her stress was the fact that Kalmon was alive. His heart was still beating. She didn't want to think about what could have happened if he had died. But thank God he was alive.

Now here she was, sitting anxiously in her Uber that was driving her to the Weill Cornell Medical Center, the private hospital located in Lenox Hill, that Kalmon was at. She couldn't stop shaking her leg as she sat in the backseat, staring out the window. Not even observing the busy New York streets was helping her calm down.

Minutes later, she finally arrived at the hospital and headed straight to the reception area. A blonde-haired Caucasian woman greeted her with a friendly smile and Azia told her her name and who she was there to see. The woman then picked up the phone to make a call before telling Azia to take a seat in the welcome area.

About fifteen minutes later, Azia got up out her seat once spotting Nolita Howard walking into the welcome area. The disheartened look on her face had Azia worried, but she still shot Nolita a friendly smile before questioning her.

"Nolita, is everything okay?"

Nolita simply gave Azia a weak smile before leaning closer to whisper, "I'm sorry, honey, I never should have made you come all this way. I've tried to talk some sense into him but... he doesn't want to see you."

Chapter Four

"What the fuck does he mean he doesn't want to see you? What kind of bitch ass nigga is he?"

Both Iman and Azia looked over at Nova after she spoke. Iman covered her mouth to hide her laughter and Azia gave Nova a surprised look before bursting into laughter and then passing the bowl of popcorn to Iman.

"He didn't want to see me and I can't force him to do something he doesn't want to do... I guess he's just hurting and doesn't want me to see that side of him right now," Azia rationalized with a light shrug.

"I get that he's going through some shit having his ex shoot him, but that doesn't mean he needs to take it out on you," Nova commented. "Niggas only know how to make problems deeper, not fix them."

After finding out that Caesar was not only married but had a child on the way, Nova had cried for exactly 24 hours. And once those hours were done, she managed to convince herself that she was a bad bitch. A bad bitch that needed to forget all about Caesar and focus on her career as an interior designer.

Nova had her own successful company that was still doing well after she started six months ago once she'd left her old job. So her main focus needed to be on her business, not on a cheating, lying ass nigga named

Caesar. She was done with him. His number was blocked, his belongings burnt and most of all, he no longer existed to her.

Azia and Iman were both glad that Nova hadn't decided to stay heartbroken over Caesar forever. She had bounced back pretty quickly and even though they knew their friend was still hurting deep down, she was doing a good job at hiding it.

The trio were currently at Iman's apartment, having an impromptu girls night with a bottle of wine and bowl of popcorn. An impromptu night that had been created courtesy of Iman, who wanted to cheer Azia up after finding out through text that she was depressed by Kalmon's shooting and him not wanting to see her today.

Kalmon's shooting was their main topic of conversation and Azia was filling the girls in on all she knew. She had found out about Jahana shooting Kalmon from Jahmai, who she'd seen coming into the hospital just as she was leaving.

After being told by Nolita that Kalmon didn't want to see her, Azia didn't bother putting up a fight. All she did was listen to Nolita's words and nodded.

"He's angry with the whole entire world right now, Azia, and I'm sorry he won't let you see him. I know he'll come around soon though and you'll be able to see him."

At the end of the day, she wasn't his girl. They were still just getting to know each other and messing around, so she didn't hold any real weight. But what she did want to know was what exactly had happened to Kalmon and she was too nervous to ask his mother, so his cousin was the next best thing. Now here Azia sat, telling her girls what had happened with Kalmon getting shot.

"Let's hope he comes back to his senses real soon and remembers what you mean to him," Iman spoke up after taking a sip from her wine. "Like his mother said, you guys are good together. He'd be a fool to mess that up."

21

"Exactly." Nova nodded.

"Jahana shooting him was so random though," Azia announced with a sad sigh. "She really had it out for him."

"Where is she now?"

"No one knows," Azia responded to Iman. "Jahmai told me about her fleeing the city with the money Kalmon came to give her right before she shot him."

"Damn. She really is cold hearted." Nova shook her head before sipping on her red wine. "That's actually my cousin. My crazy ass cousin."

"Your crazy ass cousin," Iman repeated after her. "At least we know your ass ain't as crazy as hers!"

"Hallelujah," Nova sang, sipping some more on her drink.

"Apparently she was the one who called the emergency services."

"What?" Nova's mouth now hung open. "But that doesn't make any sense... she's the one that shot his ass."

"Jahmai mentioned how the police tried to get involved and said that a woman was the one the 911 dispatcher responded to. And when the paramedics got on the scene, her apartment door was left ajar."

"So she shot the nigga, left him for dead and then suddenly had a change of heart?" Nova queried. "This ain't making any sense."

"That was what Jahmai told me." Azia shrugged before diving her hand into the popcorn bowl.

"Well damn, Jahmai sure had a lot of tea to spill to you, missy."

Azia stuffed popcorn into her mouth and shot Iman a goofy grin while doing it. Once she was done chewing, she replied to Iman's comment.

"What can I say? He likes me."

"Jahmai... that's the guy that was holding onto me at the casino? When I tried to give a good punch to the person who needed one?"

"That's the one." Azia nodded at Nova.

"Oh yeah, the fine ass nigga whispering in her ear!" Iman exclaimed.

"He whispered in her ear?"

"Yes! And when he was done she looked all smitten, like she wanted to jump on his dic—"

"Erm, I won't be jumping on anyone's dick for the rest of this year, thank you very much," Nova cut Iman off. "He was nice, but the fact that he kept holding me back was aggravating as fuck."

"You would have done something that you would have regretted later, Va. It's a good thing he did," Azia said.

"Hmm, I guess." Nova's eyes drifted down to Azia's carpeted floor momentarily before they lifted back up. "He was pretty fine though."

"Fine as fuckkkkkk," Iman sang in a tipsy voice, letting the girls know that she was definitely getting drunk... or already drunk. They all laughed heartily at Iman's antics.

Azia could feel her liquor getting to her too but she was trying to take it easy because she still had to get up early for work tomorrow.

Going into work tomorrow felt like the biggest drag after the day that Azia had just had. Kalmon not wanting to see her today had hurt her feelings, but she was trying to rationalize in her head his potential reasons. Maybe he just didn't want her to see him all vulnerable and weak on a hospital bed that he never wanted to be on in the first place. But even that reason hurt Azia deeper. If he didn't want her to see him vulnerable and weak, then how was she supposed to get to know him better? How were they to progress on whatever it was that they were doing?

The girls chopped it up for a few more hours until it was 10:30 pm. Then Azia and Nova said their goodbyes to Iman. Nova hopped in her Uber home to her apartment complex that was located fifteen minutes away, whereas all Azia needed to do was walk down to the fifth floor since she and Iman lived in the same apartment complex.

Once the girls were gone, Iman began to clear up her living room. She could feel the ground moving slightly and she released a light giggle as she picked up empty glasses. Alcohol danced in her system and she knew right now that the best remedy was sleep. She wasn't drunk, more so on the tipsy side, but the liquor flowing through her veins felt good. After tidying up the room, Iman headed straight for her bedroom about to enter until she heard light knocking on her front door.

Did one of these girls forget something just as I'm about to sleep?

Iman turned around and slowly strode over to her front door, already having a hunch that it was Azia at the door.

"Girl, whatever you forgot I can't find... Key?"

Her palms got sweaty at the instant locking of his brown eyes to hers, and her nipples hardened underneath her top. It had to be the wine in her system making her desire creep up strong. Desire for a man she had no business having despite the fact that he had been inside her once before.

"Did you see Athena take her abortion pills?"

What the... Iman looked up at him with a baffled gaze.

"Excuse me?"

"You heard what I said," he stated, walking right into her apartment like he owned the place.

"I didn't say you could come in." She watched him stalk his way through her home and head straight to her living room area, taking a seat on one of her couches. "How'd you even find out where I live?"

"Well I'm here now," he voiced, resting his right arm on her arm rest while his other arm was up on the top of her couch. He chose to ignore her question though, not needing her to know what he'd hacked into to retrieve her address.

His eyes briefly scanned her abode, taking in the feminine colors that coated her space. Pinks, whites and beiges surrounded them and they made Keon smile internally at how the colors of her home suited her perfectly.

"So answer me."

Iman stayed standing by her open door, hating how good he looked seated on her couch right now. He had on a red Nike tracksuit with white Air Force Ones gracing his feet. His hoodie was up, concealing his head only slightly because she could still see the top of his freshly cut waves.

Quickly shaking inappropriate thoughts of her sister's boyfriend, Iman shut her door and walked nearer to where he sat. Instead of sitting, she remained tall and crossed her arms against her chest while nervously looking at him.

"No, I didn't see her take them. I just came with her to her appointment as she wanted me to," she admitted.

"But you weren't in the room with her and her doctor?"

"No, I wasn't. I waited for her outside and once she was done she came out with her bag of pills."

Iman had followed her sister to her doctor's appointment but waited in the waiting room as Athena had told her to. She'd offered to come in with her but Athena had made it clear that she could handle it.

"A'ight then," Keon responded with a nod.

"Did you really end things with her?"

Iman remembered back to a couple days ago, that awkward time in her office as she silently watched Keon and her sister's relationship crumble right in front of her. All because she couldn't keep her mouth shut... or her legs.

"She's still pregnant," Keon revealed, resulting in Iman's mouth to drop wide open.

"Wait, what?"

"Yeah," he confirmed with a chuckle. "Same fuckin' reaction I had."

Iman had tried to call her sister numerous times, to try to apologize for revealing her abortion to Keon, but Athena never picked up. Or returned a single text. And it only made Iman feel bad which was why tonight she'd started drinking to help ease her guilt. It was a pointless tactic though because she still felt her guilt suffocating her. That was until Keon's announcement.

"She never went through with the abortion and when I asked her why she ain't do that shit like she planned to, she said she couldn't bring herself to kill our unborn child. I also asked her stupid ass why she'd want to do something like that in the first place, and she claimed that she was scared. Scared of giving birth again after so long and scared to have to go through the whole process again."

Keon's thoughts began to drift away to memories of the words Athena had told him. Right after he watched her pee on a pregnancy stick that he'd had one of his goons bring over to his crib.

He didn't believe her when she said she was still pregnant which was why he needed physical confirmation that he could only get by watching her. And once that pregnancy test came up positive with two lines, Keon wanted to feel happy but every single fiber of his being wanted to choke the fuck out of her for keeping it away from him in the first place.

She claimed she never meant to hurt him, but she had done exactly that. And if Iman had never revealed the apparent abortion, would she have ever told him the truth? Would she have changed her mind again and decided to kill their baby?

"I also asked her why she lied to her own sister about me not wanting a baby I never knew she had, and she said she just needed your support. That was the only way she knew how to get it."

By lying to me? Iman mused to herself. *Damn, does she really think that low of me?*

"I still think she's full of shit though and me ever trusting her again is unlikely."

"She's carrying your child, Keon. You have to trust her."

Keon's eyes swept up and down Iman's clothed body. She wore gray sweats and a white crop top. A simple fit that did nothing to keep the lustful thoughts he currently had at bay. Her red hair was currently tied back away from her face, letting those green-colored eyes of hers that had specks of sepia brown, shine more.

"Come here," he ordered, carefully watching her.

"Huh?"

"Come here, Iman."

She took him in as he sat on her couch like he owned the place. And now he was ordering her over to him like he owned her.

"I'm good over here."

"I want you over here."

"I don't need to be over there."

"I have no problems getting you and bringing you here myself," he told her simply.

Iman said nothing as her arms remained crossed against her chest. She just continued to stare him down before deciding to do as he wanted and come over to where he sat. She got closer to the couch but still refused to sit down. Fear lurked within her at what would happen if she did.

"That's still not you coming here, Iman," he said, lightly shaking his head at her.

"This is as close as we're going to get tonight," she informed him.

"Oh word?" He looked up at her with a smirk.

"Word."

Her arms were still crossed and a stern look was plastered on her pretty face.

"Keon, you've asked me what you wanted to ask me so why are you still he—"

"Because I want to be," he cut her off, getting out of his seat and walking to her.

Without her being able to run, Iman found herself being pulled into his arms and before she knew it, they were both sitting on her couch. But he was the only one actually sitting on her furniture whereas she sat... on him.

"Keon, no," she protested, trying to push him away and get up from his lap, but it was no use.

His grip on her waist was strong and his strength no match for her.

"Yes," he insisted, holding her gaze. He found himself getting lost in her eyes like he always did. He wanted to get so lost inside her that he never had to pull out to be found.

"No, Key... please," she said with a sigh, not liking how fast her heart was beating right now, and not liking how her pussy was purring at smelling his cologne. And because she was on his lap, she could feel his arousal poking her leg.

"This is wrong."

"I don't care." He pecked her exposed collarbone. "I want you."

"I don't want you," she whispered, looking away from him. Then she felt her face being turned and she was forced to stare into that handsome face of his.

"Say that shit again. Louder."

"I don't..." Her words trailed off as she realized that she couldn't even bring herself to say it with full confidence because she knew it was a lie.

"We can't do this, Key. As attracted as we are to each other, we just can't. I'm not having sex with my sister's boyfriend."

"You already had sex with me," he reminded her with a small smile. "You just didn't let me finish and give you what you needed."

A flashback of them having sex on her desk flew into her head which made the wetness flowing out of her drip faster.

"We're not finishing," she informed him, a firmness gracing her eyes. "Key, I can't do this with you... I can't do this to my sister who already hates me for telling her secret."

"A secret she never should have had in the mothafuckin' first place," he retorted.

"Still doesn't mean we're hav... mmh, Key... Key, no."

"Tell me... this doesn't... feel right," he said in between his kisses on her neck.

"It doesn't..." Iman found herself extending her neck so he could get better access on kissing her flesh. "It doesn't... shit, it does... it does."

With his strong arms still wrapped around her waist and his lips now glued to her skin, Iman couldn't control the way her body was reacting to this man. She couldn't control the desire crawling out of every aspect of her body, telling her to jump on this man right now and let him have his way with her.

"Key, please... don't make me want you."

He stopped kissing on her body and looked into her eyes.

"That's too bad because that's exactly what I intend to do."

"But what about Athena?"

"What about her?" he asked nonchalantly.

"That's the mother of your child, Key!" she protested. "The mother of your future child."

"That was supposed to be you."

"Now you're just talking shit."

"No I'm not," he fumed. "I'm dead ass."

"Well it's not me, so go to who we both know it is," she concluded, trying to get off his lap but failing miserably because of his hold on her.

"I'm not leaving you tonight, Iman. No matter what you say."

"And we're not having sex tonight, Keon. No matter how good you try to seduce me."

They both gave each other a heated stare, both refusing to break away. And it wasn't until a few seconds later that Keon moved closer to her, resting his forehead against hers. Iman shut her eyes as he did that, sighing softly. Then she felt his soft lips press against hers.

Surprisingly, she welcomed the kiss. Their mouths moved in sync and when he pushed his tongue past her lips to deepen the kiss, Iman opened all the way up for him. Their tongues happily danced, pleasuring each other in ways that words could not. Their kiss went on for a few more minutes before Keon finally pulled away.

"It's late," he spoke up. "I know you got work tomorrow so you need to get some sleep."

Iman gave him a neutral expression before nodding gently. Even though she'd been trying to convince herself that he needed to go, now that it seemed he was doing it after all, broke her heart a little. Even after saying he wasn't going anywhere tonight, he was still going.

But that was Iman's assumption being dead wrong because instead of leaving, Keon carried her up by her waist and led the way into her bedroom. He sat her down on her double sized bed, keeping locked eyes on her while he took off his tracksuit.

As each article of his clothing came peeling off his body, the more wet she got at the sight of him. He was too beautiful. Him, his chest of tattoos and those well-defined abdominal muscles of his. He was perfection personified. Perfection in the physical and everything she knew she wanted but couldn't have. He was her forbidden fruit.

As much as she was enjoying the view, she was confused as to why he was stripping when she'd made it clear they weren't engaging in coitus tonight.

"We're not having sex, Iman. I know. Relax," he said with a sexy smirk, answering her conflicting thoughts for her. "We are sleeping together though."

Once he was left in nothing but his boxers, he strolled over to her and helped her take off her clothes till she was in nothing but her panties.

Seeing her gorgeous naked body, had him fighting an internal battle to want to please her, but he fought off the urge. Instead he got under her lilac covers, looked at her observing him shyly and patted on the empty space next to him.

Iman crawled over to the spot and got under her covers, snuggling up next to him. He placed his arm around her, keeping her as close to him as he possibly could before pecking her forehead. She then shut her eyes while one hand sat on his stomach, caressing it gently as she drifted off to sleep.

What they were doing from this point forward, neither of them knew. But what they did know was that their want for one another was going nowhere. Regardless of the pregnant woman that happened to be her sister and his girlfriend.

Chapter Five

"I can't take this shit anymore. I need to get out of here."

"Now we both know you can't do that, Mr. Howard."

"I can do whatever the fuck I want to do."

"Not while you're still recovering, sir. And even though you had a successful surgery, you still need to heal. You trying to move around and be on the go like you didn't get shot twice, is only going to cause yourself more pain. You've gotta take things slow and be patient."

Kalmon stared deeply into the eyes of the nurse standing by the edge of his bed. He gave her a blank stare, feeling frustrated deep inside because he knew she was 100% right. He had to be patient, even though that's the last thing he wanted or needed right now.

"Besides, we both know your mother won't be happy to know you've left this hospital without her permission. She made it clear that I had to keep an eye on you whenever she's not here, and I'm doing exactly that, Mr. Howard."

After her words, her plump lips curved into a friendly smile as she watched him. Lavena was the nurse that had been assigned to look after him while he recovered and not only had the hospital assigned her, but his mother had taken extra care in making sure that Lavena knew to keep a very close eye on him. Kalmon already had a strong hunch that his

32

mother had slipped her some extra dollars on the side so she could report every single detail of Kalmon's activities while he lay on his hospital bed. Including the activities that involved him threatening to leave.

Lavena wasn't bad to look at all though and every time Kalmon's eyes met hers, he was reminded of her beauty. She was fair-skinned, had jet-black hair that framed her attractive face and chestnut-colored eyes. Her body was an even bigger problem though, because it couldn't be hidden underneath those blue scrubs. She was thick in all the right places, had perky breasts and an ass out of this world. Lavena was definitely a cutie so he couldn't help but lust over her.

"I'll be back to check your heart rate and blood pressure again including giving you your next dose of morphine. If you need anything at all, press your button and I'll be on my way," she said.

Knowing that he wasn't going to respond, she took one last look at him before leaving the room. Leaving Kalmon alone with his thoughts.

He had been cooped up in this hospital room for too long. It had only been ten days but still, it felt like too damn long to him. What he wanted to be able to do more than anything was find Jahana and make her pay for what she had done. She had caught him off guard, something no one was ever able to do, and now she'd run off with his cash, fled his city as if he wasn't going to snap her neck the second he laid eyes on her.

It wasn't just Jahana that dominated his thoughts. It was his brother and his part in Jahana attempting to murder him. He still wasn't sure what to believe and who to trust. If Keon really didn't have a part to play in Jahana's plan, why did she make it seem like he had? The shit just didn't make any sense to Kalmon.

Ding!

Kalmon looked over to the cabinet next to his bed, seeing his phone lighting up and he gently reached across for it.

Look, I know you hate me right now but I promise you bro, I'm gonna find that bitch and make her pay for what she's done to you.

Keon.

Believe that.

Keon.

Just focus on getting better.

Keon.

I love you bro. Never forget that.

Keon.

Without responding, Kalmon simply read over the texts from his brother. Right now he didn't want to see or speak to his brother. If his brother really wanted to prove to him that he wasn't a snake, then he would find Jahana and bring her straight to him. But for now, Kalmon would keep his distance while also making sure the goons he'd put in charge of finding Jahana were doing everything in their power to find her.

He took one last look at Keon's messages before heading through his unread text messages. He kept scrolling through, seeing the various people that had sent him messages. His business associates at the casino, Caesar, his attorney and his accountant had flooded him with messages wanting to meet up with him. Only a select few knew about Kalmon's shooting and he wanted it to remain that way. He couldn't have everyone knowing his personal life too deeply. And he didn't want niggas thinking he was weak just because he'd been shot. His body may have been wounded but his mind was still as powerful as ever. And he didn't want anyone thinking they could take advantage of him right now.

Kalmon kept scrolling through only to stop scrolling when he caught a glimpse of a name he badly missed.

Azia: *Let me know if you're coming to see me tonight.*

It was an old message and one that he'd already seen countless times before, but it still warmed his heart the same every single time.

Fuck... I miss her pretty ass.

34

He knew he'd been grimy by not allowing her to see him when his mother had invited her 'round but the truth was, he didn't want to see her. He didn't want to see anyone but Jahana with a bullet in her head.

Call him crazy, but Kalmon was out for blood. But it wasn't just his anger about wanting revenge that made him push Azia away, it was his anger about being in such a weak position. Being confined to a hospital was a weakness to Kalmon, and he never liked to show weakness. It didn't matter how much he was feeling Azia, he just wasn't comfortable with the position he was in right now. He didn't want her seeing him like this. Even his own mother and father seeing him like this pissed him off. But it was what it was. Soon, Kalmon would be out of here and hopefully Azia didn't hate him too much. He would do whatever he needed to do, to make it up to her.

* * *

"DO YOU NEED ANY HELP, HONEY?"

"No, I'm okay, thank you," Nova told the lady watching her from the checkout area.

She grabbed hold of her basket tighter and started making her way through the beauty supply store. She was running low on her products for her natural hair and decided to use this morning to purchase what she needed and run a few errands around town.

Today there was a different lady in charge of the shop and not the usual woman that she laid eyes on every time she came to the beauty supply. The woman that owned the beauty supply was a beautiful African-American woman who had a heart of gold, the main two reasons why Nova bought from her shop. It was a black-owned business, selling black-owned products and Nova would gladly spend all her coins here if she had to. Just as she got to the isle where edge control gels were, Nova heard her name being called.

"Is that my Nova?"

Nova turned around to see the one woman on her mind.

Anaya was the owner of the beauty supply store and someone Nova had grown to develop a close bond with. She truly appreciated Anaya for opening a black-owned business that Nova could come to every month to get what she needed to take care of her natural hair.

"Anaya! I thought you weren't in today?" Nova questioned her as they embraced lovingly.

"Oh I was just in the back sorting out a few deliveries with my son," Anaya explained with a friendly smile. "You here for your usual stuff?"

"Yeah," Nova said with a chuckle. "I'm running low on everything."

"Well I made sure to stock up on your favorite stuff so whatever you need, I've got you, sweetie."

"Thank you so much, Anaya."

"Anything for you, Nova. You know that."

The women both smiled at each other and just as Nova was about to ask Anaya how business was going, was when Nova heard that deep familiar voice that had made her insides turn to mush on a night that she had been devastated and livid. The night that she'd had her heart broken into a million pieces all at once.

"Ma, you've got one more delivery…"

Jahmai's words trailed off as he walked through the aisle that his mother was standing in the middle of. His mother who was standing next to the pretty woman that he had met just over a week ago.

"Jahmai, there you are," his mother greeted him happily. "Come over and meet my best customer, Nova."

Jahmai could already see the wheels spinning in his mother's head, trying to play matchmaker with the beauty standing next to her. But Jahmai had already become acquainted with this beauty and also knew of the drama she came with. The casino night had proved that all to him. It didn't matter how much of a beauty she was. With her perfect, warm caramel skin, those big brown eyes of hers, those pink, plump lips and her curly hair that he lowkey wanted to run his hands through. Or better yet, put her hair in a ponytail while she sucked a particular part of him... but that couldn't happen.

As he stepped closer to them, Nova's heart raced away but her eyes refused to tear away from his attractive face. That attractive face that she hadn't stopped thinking about since the casino night.

Coffee brown skin coated his exterior. Skin that looked smooth and perfect as ever. The bushiness of his beard was one that had enticed her from the second she laid eyes on it. She badly wished she could run her acrylic nails through it. His beard extended along his jawline and his goatee sat below his juicy lips. The small locs that Nova had seen on his head at the casino night were braided back and his sides cut into a low fade. But the thing that topped it off the most were those mahogany irises of his, invading her like he owned her alone.

"Nice to meet you, Nova."

Nova's eyes met his hand that he was now holding out for her to shake. She hadn't expected him to act like he didn't know her, like they hadn't met before but nonetheless, she decided to follow his lead.

"It's nice to meet you too, Jahmai," she replied, gently shaking his hand.

Nova wouldn't have ever guessed that Anaya was Jahmai's mother but now that she could see them both, standing side by side, she realized that they did look pretty alike. They both had the same brown complexion and mahogany pools.

Once Jahmai and Nova were done with their introductions, Jahmai informed his mother about her last delivery of the month coming tomorrow before heading back to the shop's stock room, leaving Nova and Anaya alone once more.

"So... what do you think?" Anaya questioned Nova with a smile in her eyes.

"About?" Nova threw her a dumbfounded look.

"Jahmai," Anaya answered. "I've been telling him to settle down and find a nice young woman to enjoy the rest of his life with. Something tells me that woman could be you."

Nova let out an awkward giggle before shaking her head.

"Oh I don't think I'm your son's type, Anaya."

"Are you crazy?" Anaya gave her a look of disapproval. "Of course you are. You're beautiful, smart, successful and respectful. What's not to like?"

Nova laughed awkwardly once again but decided not to answer Anaya's question. As handsome as Anaya's son was, there was just something in the back of Nova's mind telling her that Jahmai wasn't really feeling her. Especially after all the shit that had gone down at the casino night. And the fact that he acted like he hadn't met her before and like he hadn't had his strong arms around her to stop her from lashing out on Caesar, had her feeling some type of way.

Twenty minutes later, Nova had just come out of the subway and was now walking through the streets of Manhattan to her apartment building.

Azia and Iman lived on the east side of Manhattan whereas Nova lived in the upper west side of Manhattan. She had her own one-bedroom apartment that she could afford thanks to her interior design company and the inheritance she had been granted from her late auntie. The woman that had raised her and been there for her through everything.

Losing her three years ago to breast cancer had been pretty hard but Nova had no choice but to move on with her life and blossom more into the strong, independent woman her auntie had raised her to be.

One thing that Nova wanted to do was break out of her lease so that she could move to the upper east side of Manhattan where Azia and Iman lived and be closer to her girls. She would even love it if she could move into their apartment building but there were currently no apartments available for rent. For now she would wait, but it was definitely one of her goals for this year.

Once at her apartment building's entrance, Nova opened the door and stepped inside. What she needed right now was her bed. Despite it only being 4 pm and a Saturday, she'd spent her entire morning running errands and buying supplies she needed such as her hair products. She'd been back and forth through the city and now more than ever, her bed was her only desire.

"Nova."

The voice of a man that she had contemplated about murdering sounded from behind her, making her freeze in her stance. Instead of turning around, she remained looking ahead at the white staircase leading upstairs to her floor.

"Nova... baby, plea—"

"Don't call me that shit, Caesar," she snapped. "You have a baby on the way with your wife so go baby her and leave me the fuck alone."

She attempted to walk forward but the second she did was when his hand grabbed her arm.

"Don't fucking touch me!"

She immediately shook him off and turned around to face him. Allowing her to look straight into his eyes and see the same guilt that she had first seen many nights ago.

His touch made her fury mount, but it also warmed her heart at the same time. His touch had been something that she used to love, and now she hated it.

"Nova, please just let me explain."

"There's nothing to explain. You're a cheater and a liar!"

"Nova, please hear me ou—"

"You not only have a wife, but she's pregnant!" Nova yelled in his face. "She's fuckin' pregnant, Caesar!"

"Nova, I'm not with her out of choice," Caesar explained. "I had to marry her or my father would have cut me off for life. It was an arranged marriage that I had no say in whatsoever."

"I don't care!" Nova cried, feeling her lids become heavy. "You lied to me. You made me believe that you loved me when all this time you were married. You made me stop spending time with my friends and you made me fall…" The tears that she had tried so hard to keep away were now making a comeback and before she knew it, the first one slid down her cheek. And then the tears wouldn't stop flowing.

Nova didn't want him to see her cry so she turned away from him. But he had already seen the first tear drop out her eye.

"Nova, I love you," Caesar whispered, stepping closer to her. "I love you and I'm not going to stop."

By now Nova had dropped her shopping bag and was now using her hands to shield her face.

"No matter how bad you try to push me away, Nova, I'm not letting you go," he promised and grabbed one of her hands off her face.

By now he had moved from behind her and was standing right in front of her. He then removed her other hand off her face, allowing him to clearly see her face. And the more her tears fell, the more his heart broke.

"I. Love. You," he whispered one last time before pulling her close and into his arms. Nova continued to sob on his chest and even though she hated this man, her love for him was unfortunately still there. How could it not be? When he'd made love to her countless times and kissed her in places that not just any man could. When they'd spent hours upon hours together, talking about their future together. When she'd been so happy with him… how could she not love him? Loving him was all she knew.

But at the end of the day, he had still hurt her. He had crushed her in the worst way possible and Nova wasn't sure if she could ever forgive him. Him being married with a wife was one thing but to know that she was pregnant, was a whole other thing. A thing that Nova just couldn't deal with right now.

"No," she announced, lifting her head off his chest and stepping away from him. "We're done."

"Nova, please don't do this."

"No!" she yelled, giving him a vicious stare. "Stay the hell away from me!"

She then grabbed her bag off the floor and stormed off, without looking back. Whatever she had with Caesar was dead and she needed to let him go, whether she truly wanted to or not.

Chapter Six

I t was 2 am which meant that Sunday had now arrived and even
though she should have been sleeping, Azia couldn't sleep at all. It
was officially two weeks since Azia had laid eyes on Kalmon and despite
how dirty he had done her by not letting her visit him in hospital, he was
still the only person she wanted to see right now.

It didn't matter how hard she tried to distract herself with work or
spending time with her girls, Kalmon was on her brain 24/7. And she
hated how much she thought about him when she really didn't want to.
He didn't deserve to be thought about when he had hurt her.

Fuck it, you need to sleep Zi. Forget about him.

Azia pulled her gray covers over her body and shut her eyes, trying to
force herself into a deep slumber. It was only when she could feel herself
finally drifting to sleep that the sound of her phone going off was heard.

Back, back-backin' it up
I'm the queen of talkin' shit, then I'm backin' it up
Back, back-backin' it up
Throw that money over here, nigga, that's what it's for

Reluctantly, she reached across to her bedside cabinet for her phone.

Only for her heart to nearly stop at the name she could now read on her bright screen. Seeing his name made her feel a mixture of emotions all at once. From shock to anger but also confusion. *Isn't he still in the hospital recovering?* Now she was worried that it wasn't even him calling her right now but his mom trying to inform her of some bad news. *At two in the morning? Really Azia? You know damn well that it ain't his mom calling you right now. It's him.*

A part of her didn't want to pick up but she couldn't kid herself and say that she didn't wanted to hear from him. So she picked up.

"Kalmon?"

"Damn... I've missed your pretty ass voice, baby girl."

Without even being able to stop her lips from curving into a smile, Azia gave in and smiled. The sound of his deep voice melting into her ears was the cause of her happiness but also the fact that he was being affectionate.

"Kalmon, are you okay? I'm so sorry you got shot," she said with a light sigh.

"Don't be sorry for some shit you never caused," he responded coolly. "I'm good though. You in bed right now?"

"Yeah, I am."

"A'ight, put some shit on and come outside."

Azia sat up on her bed and frowned.

"Huh?"

"Come outside."

"What do you mean?"

"Come. Outside," he repeated firmly. "Culhane's waiting for you right now to drive you to me, so get dressed and go outside."

"Kalmon, it's 2 am and I'm sleeping," Azia voiced with a mean mug.

"No you ain't fuckin' sleeping 'cause you just picked up my call."

"Well I'm going to sleep now," Azia affirmed.

"No you ain't 'cause I'm seeing you tonight."

"Kalmon, no, you're no—"

"I know you're still mad at me for not letting you see me that day you came to the hospital, but that ain't got shit to do with what's happening tonight. I miss you. I wanna see you and I'm not taking no for an answer. So either get your ass outside your apartment in the next ten minutes, Azia, or be prepared to get dragged out your apartment. The choice is yours, baby."

She hated how he sexy he sounded while being so bossy and dominant. She also hated the fact that he was acting like she had a choice on the matter when clearly she didn't. But most of all she hated that she was currently climbing out of her bed and heading to her wardrobe to change out of her pyjamas.

"I'll be seeing you soon, Zi. Bring the key you have to get into my spot."

Here he was giving out orders and here she was obeying them. As if he hadn't pushed her away two weeks ago.

Ten minutes later, Kalmon's driver, Culhane, had dropped her outside Kalmon's condominium complex. Now she stood in the center of the elevator leading to the top floor. As fast as her heart was beating out of her chest, she was sure a heart attack was near. Why her nerves were this bad, she didn't understand. This was just Kalmon she was about to see. Kalmon who she hadn't seen in two weeks.

Get it together, Zi, she coached herself as she took bold strides towards his front door. With his silver key in her right hand, she placed it to the keyhole and turned it to get inside.

The second the door opened, was the exact same second she noticed him standing right on the other side.

Oh how she had missed him. It had only been two weeks but still, that felt long. Way too damn long. She melted instantly at the sight of him. Those chocolate eyes held her captive with each passing second, and she found herself breathless at the sight of him. She couldn't even utter a single word right now.

Kalmon stood tall and mighty which was a shock to her because he'd been shot. But still, his 6'5 frame was as bold and majestic as ever. He had on a loose-fitting navy t-shirt with matching navy sweatpants and was barefoot. He was also well groomed with a fresh haircut, his usual low fade and a light wavy top. And his beard sat full and ample on his light beige face. The more she took in the sight of him, the more she wanted him.

And for Kalmon it was the exact same feeling. His eyes stayed fixed on her hazel ones, his mood lifting at the fact that she was standing right in front of him. In a black coat which was open, revealing her cropped gray sweater and matching leggings. She had her natural hair up in a ponytail away from her face, and seeing her fresh faced with no make-up on right now was an absolute turn on for him. Missing her was an understatement because he hadn't just missed her, he'd been starving for her.

The both of them eventually had enough of standing in silence and just staring at each other. They both raced toward one another and grabbed hold of each other before locking lips and kissing erotically away.

Her hands went to his neck, pulling him closer whereas his went to her waist before sliding down her back to palm her ass. Their lips moved in perfect sync, not missing a beat in pleasuring each other. The way he claimed her lips had her whole body aching for him. And when his tongue gently pushed through the opening of her mouth, she yielded further for him and allowed him to dominate.

"Shit…" he whispered between their lips. "I've fuckin' missed you, Zi."

"I… mmh… I've missed you… more," she responded, pushing her body against his. but it resulted in him to groan out. However, it wasn't a familiar groan that she was used to from him and upon hearing it, she quickly broke away.

"I'm sorry, did I hurt you?"

"Nah," he said, shaking his head and pulling her back closer to him. "It's just my wounds, not you."

She cocked her head to the side and looked up at him suspiciously.

"Kal, why are you out the hospital so soon?"

"'Cause I couldn't stand being in that bitch," he explained, pressing a kiss to her lips. "I'm fine."

"You're still in pain," she informed him with a firm head shake. "You're not fine."

"I am," he insisted, looking down at her carefully. "I don't need to be laid up in a hospital bed any longer. What I need is to be at home, back to work and back with my girl. So that's exactly what I'm doing."

Her cheeks warmed at his mention of her being his girl.

"And what exactly has your mom said about you leaving the hospital early?"

Azia observed the flash of guilt in his eyes.

"She's not happy but we've come to an agreement that I don't do too much and my nurse visits every few days to clean my wounds and provide my medication," Kalmon explained before pressing another kiss to Azia's soft lips. "Speaking of my mom… you okay with her knowing about us?"

"Yeah," she answered shyly, remembering that Nolita knew about them. "She always knew about us."

"She did?"

"Yeah." Azia laughed. "She definitely knew."

"Well I'm happy you're good with her knowing. Besides, I knew she was never gonna have a problem with us being together because she loves your ass. You're her golden girl."

Azia giggled before simpering at him and just as he was about to join their lips back together, Azia pushed her head back and cocked a brow at him. Resulting in Kalmon giving her baffled eyes.

"You ain't gon' let me kiss you no more?"

"You were the one that didn't want to see me, remember?"

"And I apologize for that shit, Zi. But I didn't want you seeing me like that," he revealed.

"Why?" she asked, sliding him a guarded look.

"Don't look at me like that, Azia," he told her, noticing her expression and frowning. "I didn't mean it in a malicious way. I just didn't want you seeing me like that. I didn't want anyone seeing me like. The shit Jahana did to me... shooting me? That shit caught me off guard and had me feeling weak in the worst fuckin' way."

"So you don't want me seeing you weak?"

"A'ight, let's not act crazy like you ain't seen me weak before," he said in a low tone before sexily whispering in her ear, "You know how weak I get when I'm in that bomb ass pussy of yours."

Azia felt the center of her thighs burn up at his seductive whisper but instead of saying anything to him, she just kept looking at him with a blank look.

"Zi, baby... I just wasn't happy about where I was and how I got there. But I don't want you angry with me anymore. I know it was wrong to not let you in and I shouldn't have pushed you away. I'm sorry."

The apologetic look in his brown eyes matched his apology and for that reason, Azia found herself no longer angry at him. How could she stay mad when he had a face as gorgeous as his?

"You're forgiven," she announced with a toothy grin.

"Oh am I?" he cockily asked her, squeezing her ass cheeks in his large palms.

"Yeah, you are."

"Are you gonna show me how much you forgive me?" The fire burning between her thighs only got stronger at his words. "Huh?"

By now his head was resting in the corner of her neck and he was kissing on her skin. His beard was tickling her skin too, and she loved it. She loved feeling his body against hers, feeling his lips on her flesh and smelling his cologne that she had missed for days now.

"Yes," she confirmed before quickly remembering about how he wasn't fully healed yet. She didn't want to inflict any more pain on him. "But Kal, you're in pain. We can't have sex."

"Who the fuck said that?" He lifted his head up from her neck to look down at her with dissatisfaction. "I'm fine."

She playfully rolled her eyes at him.

"I don't want you straining yourself."

"I won't strain myself," he stated. "'Cause I'm gonna sit back and watch you work the dick that I know you've missed."

Azia gave him a coy look.

"You have missed him, right?"

She nodded submissively and Kalmon lifted his right hand to her throat, gently stroking it before running his fingers across her glossy pink lips.

"And you're gonna show me just how much you've missed him?"

She nodded once again and slowly parted her lips for him which allowed him to push his finger into her mouth. The way her lips enveloped around his index finger made the hard erection in his pants only get worse. And at this point, there was only one other thing he wanted to push past her lips and have her sucking.

"Shit, Azia."

By now her entire mouth had come down on the top half of his dick whereas the lower half was currently being twisted around with her warm hands. They hadn't even made it upstairs to his bedroom because Azia had started pulling on his sweats and boxers the second he released his finger out her mouth. He currently sat on his couch, legs wide open with Azia on her knees in front of him.

She wanted to feel him in her mouth and now she had exactly what she wanted. Her tongue worked its magic, curling and dancing around his shaft in the perfect way.

"Ahhh, damn."

His groans were telling her that she was doing everything right to him which was an extra added ego boost since she had only just started. Kalmon had loosened her hair from its hold and was now raking his fingers through her hair, putting it up in all types of ponytails like he'd become a newly qualified hair stylist.

"Look at you... fuck... sucking your dick like a pro," he commented with a groan as their eyes remained locked.

Even as she sucked and licked him, her eyes were focused on his, and he loved that shit. Those innocent eyes of hers were gazing at him. Gazing at him when they both knew that she was being the complete opposite of innocent right now.

"Shittt, baby."

The more he watched her head bob up and down and felt the tender interior of her mouth wrapped around his rod, the more he could feel his pleasure rising. Then she did the sexiest shit by sliding her mouth off him momentarily so she could spit on him, only to lick all the mess she had made.

"You bad girl," he whispered as his eyes widened at the sight of her tonguing him down nonstop.

She even pushed herself all the way down his dick, removing her hands from his base so she could swallow his long length down her throat. It was an act that had Kalmon squirming and shaking in his seat.

"Fuck! Fuck! Fuuuuuuck."

All Azia did was smile triumphantly and kept on exploring his manhood with her tongue. She used the tip of her tongue to make circular motions up and down his length before kissing it affectionately like it was her most prized possession.

"Baby... I don't want you... hurting your jaw," Kalmon spoke up in a weak tone. The confused look she gave him as she deepthroated him once more made him continue talking. "I don't cum from head."

Azia wanted to burst out laughing after his words but instead of doing that, she continued to bob her head up and down while massaging his base. *Yeah, we'll we see about that,* she mused with an internal smile and a stronger determination to get Kalmon to climax. But Kalmon could already read her mind and didn't want her getting her hopes up.

"Baby, trust me I do... uhhhhhhh, goddamn it!"

Azia observed as Kalmon's head tilted all the way back against his couch. She loved the fact that he had suddenly cried out in ecstasy and she knew exactly why he had too. It was because she had suddenly started rubbing on his gooch while sucking on his balls. When Azia had her mind on a task, she didn't stop until that task was completed and that's exactly what she intended to do with making Kalmon cum.

"Azia, shit... sto... stop."

He was telling her to stop but they both knew he was a liar. The biggest liar. The very last thing he wanted her to do was stop, and Azia wasn't making any plans on doing so. She continued rubbing against his gooch area and sucking hard on his balls before lifting her lips to his gooch area and replacing her hands with her tongue.

"Fuck Azia, I'm, ugh.. I'm gonna fuck you up."

She could only smile harder to herself and eagerly pressed her tongue against his gooch while using her hands to caress his balls. She was honestly having the time of her life right now.

Yeah, you're my little bitch tonight. You like this shit too much, huh? she thought to herself as she watched his teary eyes. *I'm going to make you cum, Kal, and prove to you that you can cum from head. Only with me though.*

Giving head was so fun to her and it wasn't something she did often so when she did do it, she went all out. She was even moaning happily while sucking him off, only making him more horny and making him part his lips wider to release his moans.

Before Azia knew it, Kalmon lifted her head up using her hair and pushed her mouth back down on his dick. Then he began fucking her mouth by pumping her mouth up and down his length. In and out it popped out her mouth, making him groan louder and louder. Azia had no control whatsoever by this point and her nose felt runny, her eyes were watery as fuck and her mouth was filling up more and more with his pre-cum and her saliva.

"This is what you wanted right?" he asked her with groans, still fucking her mouth. "This is what you fuckin' wanted? For me to cum? Well you got it. You f-fuckin'... aghhhhh... you fuckin' got it... Yeah, that's right... eat up all this mothafuckin' dick."

Faster and faster, he pushed her head up and down his shaft and the more he did, the more wet Azia could feel herself getting. His manhood was fat and filled with cum so they both knew that any minute now, he was about to explode in her mouth.

But instead of releasing into her mouth, Kalmon pulled her hair up, grabbed her throat, brought her face directly to the tip of his dick and quickly began rubbing on his shaft with his other hand.

"Ahhhh, fuuuuuuuck."

Azia shut her eyes but opened her mouth to welcome his warm release that landed on her face and in her mouth. It also hit the sides of her mouth, her nose and even her damn forehead. Once he had finished ejaculating on her, Kalmon leaned forward and began licking the remnants off her pretty face. He didn't stop licking until every single drop of his cum was gone off her skin. Then he kissed down her face until his thick lips landed on hers and he devoured her mouth with deep strokes of his tongue, allowing his cum to mix with their sloppy kiss.

"You... freak," Azia called him between their embrace seconds later.

"Says the... freak herself," he said before pulling away from her. "You made me cum from head, something no woman has ever done."

"No one?"

"No fuckin' one," he confirmed. "I'm the only nigga you make cum from head, a'ight? The only nigga that gets to fuck your mouth, buss on your face and lick all that shit off. No one else."

"No one else," she promised, pecking his lips once more.

Minutes later, both lovers were completely naked, still on Kalmon's couch but more than ready to engage in a long needed sex session.

Azia gently guided herself down Kalmon's erection. She held onto his base and slowly pushed him deep within her walls, moaning as she did so.

"Oh my... shit..."

The tightness that he had missed coating the exterior of his dick was finally back, and all Kalmon could do was groan with great satisfaction while leaning forward slightly to kiss Azia's back. She was currently positioned on top of him but with her back facing him, so in the reverse cowgirl position. Giving Kalmon the perfect view of her ass moving on top of him.

Spank!

Azia whimpered at the connection of his palm to her butt.

"Uhhh, Kal."

"Shut up and show me how much you forgive me," he demanded.

"Yes, baby," she obeyed, beginning to move her body up and down for him.

It was only a few seconds into Azia beginning to ride him that the sound of barking was heard. Both Azia and Kalmon looked to the right-hand side of the room to see Diamond watching them. Even though she was just a puppy, Azia felt mortified that Diamond had woken up out of her sleep right now and was watching the both of them. She was like a little kid catching her parents in the act of something extremely private. Azia stayed now stationary on Kalmon's dick.

"Diamond, get your dumb ass out of here!" Kalmon bellowed, but Diamond stayed put watching the naked pair.

"Diamond, don't make me tell your ass again. Go back to sleep! You ain't supposed to be up right now. Get!"

Kalmon grabbed a pillow off the couch and chucked it at her which made her run out the living area back to her room.

"I'm over here about to feel mommy ride daddy's dick in the best way and you over here tryna interrupt!" he yelled through clenched teeth. "With your disrespectful ass! You can forget about watching Peppa Pig tomorrow morning too."

Diamond started barking from her room, making Azia laugh at her antics.

"Shut your ass up and sit your ass down back in your bed, D. Now!"

Diamond barked one last time before finally stopping.

"You're too strict on her, Kal. Leave my baby alone."

"If I leave your baby alone…" His words faded off his lips as he looked down at the sight of Azia beginning to go all the way down his shaft so that it was buried within her. "Shit… she'll be spoiled and never listen to her daddy."

"She's already spoiled because of you," Azia reminded him, holding onto his thighs as she lifted herself up and down his dick.

"True, but if I leave her she'll be spoiled even more. I gotta remind her of… of who's in charge. The same way I remind you all the time."

"Remind who?" Azia turned around to give him a skeptical look.

"You," Kalmon stated with a smirk before moving his hand to the front of Azia's body, between her thighs where he could play with her clit.

"You're not… You're not… ahhhh, shit Kal."

"I'm not what?" he questioned her, rolling his long fingers around her clit which resulted in pleasure overtaking her soul, making her cease in bouncing on him, much to his displeasure. "Did I tell you to stop riding me? Huh?"

"Kalmonnnnn, ugh!"

Azia couldn't control her moans and whimpers at this point because of the way Kalmon's fingers were toying with her clit.

"Did I fuckin' tell you to stop?"

"No, baby!"

Spank!

He slapped her cheeks before ordering, "So carry on then."

"Yes, baby."

And that right there reminded Azia exactly who was in charge. It was him all the way and she absolutely loved it. He could be in charge of her any day, any time.

Chapter Seven

"Oh my... Kalmon, are you trying to get me pregnant?" Azia queried with a deep sigh.

"Maybe," he whispered before cupping her breasts and latching his mouth onto her right brown nipple. He began to suck on her hard bud like he needed it to survive.

His dick was still nestled inside her and they'd both just come down from their first orgasm of the morning. They'd been going at it since the early hours of this morning when Azia had come over to Kalmon's.

She placed her hand to the back of Kalmon's wavy head, holding it carefully while he licked and tasted her nipples.

"I really missed you, Kalmon... like I was so damn scared when your mom told me about your shooting."

He released her bud from his mouth and gazed up at her pretty face.

"You have nothing to be scared about though, beautiful. I'm with you and I'm not going anywhere. I promise."

She gave him a simper before replying, "You better not."

"How could I ever leave a beauty like you?"

Azia's heart warmed immediately at his words.

"But seriously though, Kal. I'm so glad you're okay. I can't believe Jahana shot you. When Jahmai told me, I couldn't believe it."

Kalmon became silent after her statement and attempted to get back in the mood by wrapping his lips back around Azia's wet nipple.

"Like, why would she do something like that to you?"

Kalmon removed his lips off her chest and slid himself out of her. He rested on his back and looked up at his white ceiling, sighing deeply. Here he was trying to keep them both in the mood, but here she was bringing up shit that he really didn't want to talk about.

"She could have killed you, Kalmon."

"And you don't think I know that shit?" he asked, glaring over at Azia.

The defensive glare in his eyes wasn't one that she was expecting at all.

"I know you know, but I just can't believe it. She really shot yo—"

"I really ain't tryna talk about that bitch right now," he cut her off. "She means nothing to me."

Azia stared silently at him and decided to simply nod with understanding. Then she slowly began moving out of the king sized bed.

"Azia… Azia, don't." He reached for her under the covers.

"No, it's fine. I should start getting ready to go," she said, trying to shake his grip from her arm.

"Go where? You ain't going anywhere unless it's you going up and down on this dick again."

Azia still tried to pull away from him, and it broke his heart a little.

"I don't want you to go, Zi. Stop that shit." He pulled her back towards him. "I haven't been with you for two weeks and now you want to go? You must be outta your damn mind."

"I don't want to stay if you're gonna push me away continuously. I'm tryna have a serious conversation with you and here you are dismissing me and shit," she voiced, looking over at his chest of drawers rather than him.

"Baby," he called to her, pulling her chin and making her look at him. "I'm not pushing you away. Talking about Jahana makes me angry and when I'm with you, I don't want to be angry. You make a nigga happy and I don't want anything to ruin that."

She was smitten by his words and decided to look deeper into his mesmerizing eyes again.

"Say you'll stay?" he queried, pressing his lips to her neck and planting sweet kisses on her skin.

"I'll stay," she promised, placing her arms around him and staying as close to him as possible.

* * *

"I SWEAR on everything I love, I would never set up my own brother," Keon testified, looking across at his cousin lifting his blunt to his lips. "My own flesh and blood? That shit don't even sound right."

"I believe you, Key," Jahmai admitted after letting out his smoke. "At first I feared the worst, but no Howard man would do shit like that. You're not a snake."

"Exactly," Keon affirmed. "Never have been and I never will be."

"I just wish Kal wasn't so damn stubborn, man."

"He wouldn't truly be my brother if he wasn't," Keon responded with a light shrug. "I know exactly what I have to do though."

"And what's that?" Jahmai took one last pull from his blunt before placing it on its ash tray to the side of him.

"I gotta find that bitch, Jahana, and deliver her straight to my brother. He wants her dead and so do I. What she did was foul as fuck, and she needs to pay for that shit."

"And she will no doubt," Jahmai confirmed with a nod. "You got any leads on her yet?"

"Nah, not yet..." Keon's words came to a halt at the sound of his phone vibrating on his lap. "She can't hide forever though."

"Facts," Jahmai voiced.

Keon looked down at his text notification from one of his goons.

No word yet boss. Still searching.

Unknown.

Keep me posted, he texted back before scrolling through his messages to find the name belonging to the woman he desired the most right now.

You having a good day MaMa?

Send.

The owner of the name read his message and couldn't help but break into a shy smile as she read it.

Yes.

Send.

Seconds later his response came shooting through.

That's good.

Aren't you gonna ask me if I'm having a good day?

K.

Are you having a good day Key?

Send.

I'm having a great day now that I'm texting you beautiful.

K.

She sent him a smiley face emoji and attempted to type back a response until she sensed movement enter her office.

"Those bathrooms of yours really are super clean," Athena announced, stepping into her sister's office and sauntering over to the white desk. "Your cleaners really do a good ass job."

Iman quickly placed her phone on do not disturb and turned her phone upside down as she watched her sister take a seat on the empty velvet chair on the other side of her desk.

"Athena look... I'm so sorry about what I did. I never intentionally meant to tell Key, it just kinda slipped out."

"How does me having an abortion just slip out?" Athena asked with an arched brow.

"He noticed my anger towards him at the casino night and wanted to address it," Iman explained, looking away to stare down at her closed MacBook. "And when I continued being standoffish it... it..."

"It slipped out," Athena finished her sister's fading words for her. "Right?"

Iman looked back into her sister's chestnut-colored eyes, seeing the annoyance she had for her sparkling within them. But as quickly as Iman saw it, it flashed away.

"I'm glad you told him."

Iman rapidly blinked at her sister's sentence.

"You are?"

"Yeah, I am," Athena revealed. "Because the truth is out and he knows that I'm carrying his child."

Athena then placed her hand on her stomach and gently rubbed it.

"I was never going to go through with an abortion."

"But why did you lie about Key telling you to get one in the first place?" Iman questioned her sister.

"Because I was scared," Athena said meekly. "Childbirth ain't no joke."

Iman stared silently at her sister, not really having a response to say back to Athena. She didn't know the pain of childbirth because she'd never experienced it. So she couldn't exactly relate.

"That's not something I'd expect you to understand though, sis."

Iman didn't like the tone her younger sister had just spoken to her in, but she chose to overlook it. At the end of the day, she'd outed Athena's secret and was trying to get her to forgive her.

"You're right," Iman stated. "And again, I apologize for everything."

Everything but Keon sliding himself inside you right here on this desk, huh? Ain't that right, Iman?

Iman shook her guilty thoughts away and observed Athena's lips curving into a small smile.

"And I forgive you, Iman. How can I not forgive my own flesh and blood?"

Iman returned her smile but behind it, she felt nothing but guilt. Guilt that was burning through her soul and taking over her mind.

"How about we go grab dinner together?" Athena suddenly suggested. "You know I'm eating for two now and this baby sure can work up an appetite."

"Sure, why not," Iman replied before querying, "How far along are you by the way?"

"About six weeks," Athena stated with a simper. "I'm actually really excited."

Iman returned her smile but said nothing in response.

"Can I grab some red velvet cupcakes from the front before we go?"

"Sure thing. They're on me so don't worry about paying."

"Are you sure?" Athena gave her sister an unsure look.

"Yeah, positive."

"Awww, thanks sis. You're the best!"

Iman continued to smile and got up out of her seat the same time as Athena. Thinking that Athena was about to walk towards the exit, Iman made her way to follow her until she noticed that Athena was making a beeline towards her. Once directly near her sister, Athena immediately pulled her close and embraced her.

"I love you so much, sis. And I'm sorry I lied about the abortion. I never should have put you through that shit. But thank you so much for being there for me as the amazing older sister that you are. I love you," Athena concluded, hugging her sister tighter.

"…I love you too."

The sisters then finished embracing one another before making their way out of Iman's office. They then picked up Athena's cupcakes, before heading to Athena's Mercedes parked outside.

Thirty minutes later, the sisters pulled up to Café China, one of the best Sichuan restaurants in the entire city. The sisters loved this restaurant a lot and hadn't been in a while, so it made sense for them to be here right now.

While they dined together, Athena was the one doing all the talking about how excited she was for her baby on the way and starting a new journey with Key. Whereas all Iman found herself doing was eating and remaining silent. Simply throwing nods and fake smiles her sister's way. Fake smiles that she could only muster up due to the fact that she wanted to appear happy for her sister. But appearances and actually being happy were two very different things.

How did life get this complicated? Iman mused to herself as she pushed her key through her door and stepped into her home.

"Yeah, lemme put all that shit on hold for now."

She heard his deep, heavenly voice before seeing him, and her heart instantly skipped a beat.

"Yeah, for sure. No more new clients though, we've got enough already."

Iman hung up her denim jacket and kicked off her black Vans before heading down the dark corridor leading to her bedroom.

"Did we get the new designs for that gaming app?"

Hearing him talk about his business was such a turn on for her right now. He had one of the best app developing companies in the game right now, and everyone knew it.

"A'ight, cool. Email me the PDFs and I'll..."

Keon's words trailed off as he turned to see her standing in the doorway of her bedroom. Seeing her standing there looking so pretty made elation race through his veins.

"I'll check them out... A'ight, bye."

He ended the call and placed his phone on her lamp stand before inching over to where she stood. Without saying a word, he grabbed her waist and pressed his lips to hers, giving her a sweet peck before releasing her.

"Hey."

"Hey," she greeted him breathlessly. That was the effect he had on her without even trying. He made her breathless and weak in the knees.

"I missed you," he whispered, pressing a kiss to her forehead.

"I missed you too," she admitted, closing her eyes and sighing softly. Then she lifted her arms to hold him, hugging him tightly and resting her head against his chest.

"You ready for bed, MaMa?"

MaMa.

It was the nickname he had given her. Simple, yet it was everything to Iman.

Her eyes fluttered open and she looked up at him only to nod in confirmation to his query. Going to bed really was the best part of her day because she got to sleep in his arms. They still hadn't had sex since that day in her office over two weeks ago, but it didn't matter. Sure it was hard for the both of them, more so Keon who went to bed with an erection and woke up with an even bigger one. But the intimacy of them falling asleep in each other's arms and waking up together was something indescribable. Something pure that they didn't want to end or plan to end anytime soon.

"A'ight, let's get to bed," Keon concluded, kissing her lips one last time.

Chapter Eight

"Look me in my fuckin' eyes while I suck on your pussy. I wanna see your pretty lil' face."

"Kal... please... I'm gonna be late... be late for w-worrrrrrk!"

"And I actually don't give a fuck," he retorted, pushing his two fingers deeper inside her. "Do what I say and you won't be late."

And after speaking, his eyes stayed locked on hers while his lips stayed locked on her wet folds. Flicking his tongue up and down her clit while his fingers kept thrusting within her walls.

"Mmmh, Kal... mon!" she cried out his name while doing as he asked by staring straight at him. Staring so deep as if she was trying to find his soul. Here she was trying to find his while he snatched hers with his talented yet deadly tongue.

"Oh my... Oh my... Kal!"

Her whispers only increased in volume as his tongue replaced his fingers and dived into her tightness. The warmth of his tongue exploring her felt out of this world. A feeling that she would never get sick of. Ever.

Kalmon's hands were now stuck to her thighs, keeping them glued to his shoulders. He didn't want her trying to run away from the ecstasy that he was providing her with this morning. She couldn't run from this.

"Fuck, Kal… baby… ahhhhhhhhhhhhh!"

Her hands grabbed the back of his head, pushing him deeper than he already was and giving her perfect leeway to ride his tongue and entire face.

Kalmon's bulge only got harder at her actions and moans. And the faster she grinded her moist center on his face, the more her delicious juices coated the hairs of his beard.

"Kalmonnnn!"

Within a few minutes, her nut came exploding right into his mouth and he lapped up every drop, not wanting to waste a single drop of her. Once she had stopped shaking and fully recovered from her orgasm, Kalmon kissed her inner thighs before questioning her.

"See, that wasn't so hard now was it, baby?"

Azia scoffed at him before bursting out into laughter and lifting her legs off his shoulders.

"Kal, I'm late now because of you."

"No you ain't," he said, stroking her warm legs. "You're sleeping with your boss' son, remember? You can come in whenever you like."

She burst out into more laughter, playfully pushing his chest before sliding to the top of his mattress, trying to get away from him.

"And where do you think you're going?" He grabbed her left ankle, stopping her from moving. "You think we're done?"

"Kalmonnn," she whined. "I gotta get going. Seriously!"

She gave him a stern look before breaking into a simper when she saw him sexily biting his lips at her. As if he hadn't tasted her just minutes ago.

"Quit looking at me like that."

"Like what?" he teased. "Huh?"

"When I get back from work, I promise I'm all yours."

"All mine?"

"Yes," she promised, watching him lustfully.

"A'ight." He shot her a simple nod before letting go of her ankle. "We're going out for dinner tonight, Zi."

"Sounds good."

"And I'm having my dessert as soon as we get back home."

Azia nodded in agreement.

"I'll come pick you up from work," he declared before quickly adding, "Don't worry, boss, Culhane will be the one doing the driving, not me. This is what I pay him for, right?"

Seeing her frown told him of what she was thinking without her even saying it. He knew she wasn't a fan of him doing too much, especially since he was still healing.

"That's what I like to hear," Azia boldly commented before rolling out of his bed.

Seeing her dressed in a slim-fitting navy dress to work made him wish she didn't have to leave him so soon. They spent every day together and it was only for work that Azia left him, or to spend time with her family or her girls. And still with how much time they spent together, Kalmon still didn't like seeing her leave him.

"I'll be seeing you later tonight, Mr. Howard."

"Damn straight," he concluded, kissing her one last time.

Just as their kiss ended and she began to walk away from him, Kalmon spanked her ass and threw her a sexy smile when she looked back at him innocently.

Once she was gone, Kalmon was left alone with Diamond. She sat on his lap watching *Peppa Pig* while he scrolled through his iPhone. Jahana was still nowhere to be found and surprisingly, she hadn't cashed his check that he had given her. She probably knew that the second she cashed it, Kalmon would be onto her location because checks could be traced, and he was waiting for her to cash it so he could finally have her ass. But for now he had to do the waiting game and leave his goons to their job of sniffing her out. Eventually a wave of tiredness overcame Kalmon's body making him drift off to sleep.

Fuck where your hoes at
Or where your Rolls at
Where your backbone, nigga, where your code at?
Where your down since day one real bros at?

It was the voice of Nipsey Hussle that woke him up out his slumber and Diamond's slumber too, who had fallen asleep on his lap.

Kalmon turned to the side to see his phone sitting on the couch space next to him, and seeing the time was 4 pm let him know he'd been out for a while. Azia had left him at around 8 am.

Shit, a nigga been napping for that long?

The next thing he spotted was the caller ID.

"Yo," he greeted his casino manager before yawning.

"Kalmon! Boss… we have a problem."

Kalmon's face contorted with irritation.

"A problem? What kind of fuckin' problem?"

"It's the casino," Caesar blurted out in a panicked tone, making every muscle in Kalmon's body tense up. He already knew whatever Caesar had to say wasn't something he was going to like. At all.

"The casino's been robbed."

Chapter Nine

R ed was all Kalmon could see right now. It didn't matter that he was looking into the swollen eyes of Caesar because all Kalmon could see was red.

"Explain this shit to me one more mothafuckin' time."

Caesar let out the breath he was holding before obeying Kalmon and explaining the situation again.

It had been a normal Tuesday at the casino. As manager, it was Caesar's job to get in early to make sure that the casino had been cleaned thoroughly by the hired cleaners and to start making a mental list of all the things he needed to assign the employees to do for the day. It was also his job to organize, plan and direct all the gaming operations in the casino. To put it simply, his job was to manage.

Caesar also had access to all the money that moved through the casino floor. He knew all the codes for the top secret vaults, had security access to the vaults and knew about moving day. His knowledge was something he had because he had earned Kalmon's trust. Something that was very hard to do. It hadn't been easy but Caesar had proved his loyalty. He'd proved it, but for Kalmon to now be hearing of the predicament the casino was in on moving day had him questioning everything he thought he knew about Caesar's loyalty to him.

Moving day was the one day out of the month that a small percentage of the money held in the casino's vaults was moved to their main bank, JP Morgan, located in Midtown Manhattan. The main reason for moving day was because the casino made too much money on a daily basis and not all that money could be kept in physical cash because Kalmon had various employees that needed to be paid. He also had bills to pay for the casino, to keep the lights on in this place, including paying the IRS.

Moving day was something that Caesar oversaw with heavily armed guards who protected him while he moved bags of money into the back of a black SUV. An SUV that was driven by one of the guards and followed by each guard in separate vehicles. It didn't happen at the same date every month too, and only happened when Kalmon gave the word for it to happen. Every single moving day had gone off without a hitch.

So for Caesar to now be sitting in front of him and spewing out the events of what had taken place an hour ago, Kalmon wanted to shoot every single employee on sight right now. All four of the armed guards who protected Caesar were dead. Caesar had been attacked and given two swollen, puffy eyes, a busted lip, a cracked nose and bruised skin.

2.5 million.

That's how much money had been stolen from the casino. It wasn't even the money that phased Kalmon. That was chump change to him. What bothered him was the fact that someone had the audacity to steal from him. Stealing from a Howard? That was a death wish, no doubt. Kalmon just wanted to know who he needed to put a bullet through the heart of. That's it.

Every single dollar bill that passed through the casino had a tracking device embedded in the currency bands that held the bills in place. And any minute now, Kalmon would know the exact location of the idiots who had been dumb enough to rob him.

"I don't know how this shit could have happened, boss."

Kalmon sat in front of Caesar, sizing him up as he spoke to him. Even with what had happened to Caesar, Kalmon didn't trust him one ounce. For the robbery to have gone as smoothly as it had with Caesar still alive, Kalmon smelled a rat. A big one.

He hoped to God that this wasn't an inside job. He prayed that for Caesar's sake, he wasn't involved in the robbery. Because if he was, Kalmon was going to cut his head off. And hang it up on the walls of his office.

"Sir."

Kalmon kept his unwavering eyes on Caesar, trying to find a glimpse of guilt or fear within them. But all he could see within Caesar was pain from his injuries. He motioned for the woman who had called his name to come closer to him.

"We've traced the money."

Kalmon's eyes stayed stuck on Caesar's for a few more seconds before he looked over at Kennedy, his data analyst, with her iPad in hand. She then passed the screen over to him and Kalmon looked down at the bright screen to see a map with a flashing blue circle.

He tapped on it and an address popped up. The second his eyes read the first line of the address, his jaw tightened and fury thundered through him.

Both Caesar and Kennedy were immediately taken aback when Kalmon got out of his seat and chucked the iPad against his office wall causing its screen to immediately shatter.

"My own fuckin' brother!" he shrieked, clenching his fists. "That stupid mothafucka. I'm going to kill his dumb ass!"

Without even explaining anything to a confused Caesar and Kennedy, Kalmon stormed out of his office with only one task in mind: To murder his younger brother.

Chapter Ten

K eon's eyes landed on his vibrating phone.

When I die, put my money in the grave
I really gotta put a couple niggas in they place
Really just lapped every nigga in the race
I really might tat "Realest Nigga" on my face

Spotting Athena's name on his screen made Keon quickly silence his phone and bury himself back into work. Right now he needed to approve these last finishing design touches from his lead designer on the new gaming app that his company had been paid to create for Sony.

Talking to his baby mama was honestly the last thing he wanted to do right now. That's all she was to him these days. His baby mama. The only reason he still was in a relationship with her, if that's what you wanted to call it anyways, was because of his seed currently growing inside her. That was it.

Her whole scheme to abort his baby behind his back but not actually going through with it was something that had pissed him off beyond anything in the entire world. He couldn't trust her, he couldn't stand to be around her and he wasn't sure if he was ever going to forgive her.

How could he? She hadn't exactly carried out her evil plot, but the fact she'd thought about doing it in the first place was a problem for Keon.

Ding!

Keon looked across his desk to his phone to see the name of the woman who brought him butterflies. Not even Athena had ever given him butterflies.

I'm not free tonight Key. I'm going out.

MaMa.

Keon: *Going out where?*

Her response came shooting in five minutes later making his face get hot.

MaMa: *Out.*

Keon: *Out where?*

MaMa: *With a friend.*

Keon: *Is this the type of friend that stands when they pee or sits down on the seat?*

MaMa: *A friend.*

Keon: *So he stands.*

Keon: *Is this a damn date?*

MaMa: *He's simply taking me out Key.*

Keon: *It's a fucking date.*

Keon: *Are you tryna get fucked up?*

MaMa: *Key don't.*

Keon: *No but are you tryna get fucked up?*

Keon: *Fuck your date.*

Keon: *You ain't going no fucking where.*

Keon: *You better be home when I get there and ready for bed.*

MaMa: *No I'm going out.*

Keon: *Oh word?*

MaMa: *Yes!*

MaMa: *He's just a friend.*

MaMa: *Besides, what's it got to do with you?*

MaMa: *You ain't my man.*

Keon: *I'm gonna fuck yo....*

Before Keon could finish typing and eagerly press send, Athena's name appeared on his screen once again. Out of annoyance for what Iman had revealed to him, he picked up.

"What, Athena?"

"Baby," Athena greeted him softly despite the fact that he'd snapped on her. "Baby, I've been trying to get through to you."

"Why?"

"Someone dropped bags of money in front of the house," she explained, making Keon rise up out his seat. "A lot of money too."

"What do you mean?"

"I found like four bags of money dropped outside our door. Someone rang the doorbell and when I came to answer it, there they were."

What the fuck? Keon mused, in disbelief about what Athena was telling him right now. No one but family knew where his crib with Athena was located. No one.

"I'm on my way home," he announced, moving away from his desk.

"And baby… this time when you come home, can you please stay the night? I really miss falling asleep in your arms…"

Keon said nothing with his phone pressed to his ear as he walked to the exit.

Of course, Athena wanted him to stay the night when for the past few weeks he never stayed at home. He never slept in their bed and barely spent time with her anymore. The only time he spent was with his son, but Athena wasn't even an afterthought.

"I'm on my way," he reported simply, choosing to ignore her question and end the call.

While he drove in his Bugatti Chiron, all Keon could think about was who the hell knew where his three-year-old laid his head to rest every single night? Who had the balls to drop bags of money on his doorstep like they'd paid him for a job that was unbeknownst to him?

None of this shit was making any sense to Keon, but he was hoping that when he made it home, everything would make sense. The only thing on his mind right now was getting to the bottom of this shit. This shit that was too random and not making any sense to him.

Keon pulled up to his driveway, parked his Bugatti outside his garage and got out his car ready to get to the bottom of whatever the fuck was going on right now.

It was only when he reached into his back pocket for his key that he heard the squealing of tires and he turned around to see a familiar Bentley SUV pulling into his driveway. Instead of parking the Bentley right next to Keon's Bugatti, Kalmon positioned it behind Keon's car and got out with the engine still running.

"Kal?" Keon greeted his brother with a mixture of confusion but gladness at his presence. He failed to notice the deadly glare in Kalmon's eyes but the closer Kalmon approached him, the more Keon could not only see his brother's rage but he could feel it. "You goo—"

"No, I ain't fuckin' good!" Kalmon exploded, stalking over to where Keon stood a short distance from his front door. "You stole from me, huh?"

"Stole from you?" Keon squinted at his brother, remaining stationary even as Kalmon stormed over to him. "Nigga, I have no idea what you're talking about but you need to chi—"

Pow!

The solid blow of his brother's fist landed right in the middle of Keon's face. Resulting in him stumbling backwards and groaning out in agony.

"Kal! What the fuck, man!"

"You stole from me," Kalmon said through clenched teeth, drawing nearer to Keon. "You fuckin' stole from me!"

Pow!

Another blow landed on Keon's face and from that point onwards, he'd had enough. He'd let Kalmon get his first punch in but now that he had done it again, Keon wasn't having it.

"Nigga touch me again, and it's about to be a mothafuckin' problem," Keon snapped, wiping his now bloody nose.

"I guess it's a mothafuckin' problem then," Kalmon voiced with a light shrug and launched at his brother once again.

The two brothers came to blows. Hit after hit came flying from both parties and as much as Keon didn't want to fuck his brother up, especially when he knew he was still recovering from his shooting, Kalmon had left him with no choice.

No words were uttered between them. Their hands did all the talking. Punch after punch kept coming both their ways and both of them got good hits in. Noses were being cracked and becoming bloody. They both had immense strength from the muscles they carried so they were both delivering powerful hits. Eventually, Kalmon was able to get his brother in a headlock, continuously hitting his head and fucking him up.

"You fuckin' stole from me! Your only brother? I'm gonna kill you."

"I don't... I don't know what the hell you're talkin' about!"

"You mothafuckin' liar!"

Keon was able to get one up on Kalmon and got out of the headlock he was in, defending himself by administering blows to his brother's face. He was trying to hit Kalmon anywhere but where he had been shot. But Kalmon was testing his patience indeed.

"Key! Kal! Stop! Stop it! Please, stop!"

It wasn't long until Athena who was inside had come out upon spotting Keon's car parked outside through the window. Then she had spotted Kalmon and when punches were being thrown, she rushed downstairs as fast she could.

Now she was pulling Keon back by his shirt and trying to get in the middle of the boys.

"Please, both of you stop!" she pleaded, her eyes misting with tears. "What the hell are you guys doing!"

"Oh, so you got your girl to come save your bitch ass, huh?" Kalmon let out a callous chuckle as he watched Keon struggle to get away from Athena.

Keon wasn't exactly struggling. It was just that his anger was pulsating through every part of his body and he was afraid of touching Athena. He didn't want to hurt her.

"Athena, move."

"No, Key! Both of you need to relax,"

"Ain't no one relaxing when I've just been fuckin' robbed by your nigga," Kalmon fumed.

"What?" Athena's mouth dropped open as she stood firm in the center of the men, trying her hardest to keep them apart.

"Don't act dumb, Athena," Kalmon berated her. "Your ass probably helped him hide the money."

"What money?" Athena questioned him. "If you're talking about the money that was left on our doorstep an hour ago, it's inside and Keon only found out about it not too long ago."

"That's what I was tryna tell his dumbass but he wouldn't listen," Keon spoke up, mean mugging Kalmon.

"Man, shut your ass up! Why have bags mysteriously been dropped at your house? Bags of money from my casino? Huh? I'll tell you why. 'Cause you're a fuckin' snake, that's why!"

"That ain't true," Keon testified with a hurt look in his eyes.

His hurt stemmed from the fact that Kalmon actually believed his brother was a snake. Keon could see it in his eyes that he believed his own lie, and that broke his heart more than anything.

"Kal... I swear on everything I didn't steal from you. I wouldn't..." Keon's words paused as he felt his eyes suddenly become moist with tears and his voice got stuck in his throat. "I-I wouldn't do that shit bro. I love you."

Keon was trying his hardest to convince his brother of his innocence, but the disgust within his brother's eyes told him that Kalmon didn't believe him. And if his look didn't tell Keon that, his last words sure as hell did.

"You're dead to me," Kalmon concluded before spitting on the floor in front of both Athena and Keon. Then he turned around and headed to his car without looking back once. Athena slowly turned around to look at Keon and saw a tear drop out his eye.

I've really lost my brother, Keon mused to himself as he watched Kalmon drive off. Now more than ever, Keon felt crushed. And he wasn't sure how things were ever going to get better again. If they were ever going to get better. The bond he had with his brother was truly broken.

Chapter Eleven

1 Week Later

"K ally, pick up my calls. I've been trying to get through to you. Stop thinking you can simply text me and not answer my calls. I'm your mother for Christ's sake, and I want to hear your voice. Don't make me come to your house and whoop your ass. Call me back, Kally. Please."

"Son, I don't know what's happened but you need to call me. You've closed your casino down and fired all your employees? What the fuck is wrong with you, boy? Call me the fuck back or I'ma let you know what the fuck it is... Just speak to me, son. I love you. Bye."

Baby... it's been a week since I've heard from you. You cancelled on our dinner plans last week and things just feel weird between us. Are you okay? Just let me know you're good 'cause you got me worried about you. Call me tonight? I miss you.

Azia.

Yo. Hit me up, Kal. I know something happened between you and Key. He ain't telling me shit and you keep dodging my calls. Don't make me come find you nigga. Call me.

Jahmai.

From his mother, his father, his cousin and even Azia trying to get in touch with him, Kalmon just wanted to be left alone and most of all, he wanted to disappear. He didn't want to be in New York anymore because he didn't want anyone trying to find him.

The past week had been him just reflecting and carrying out plans that he thought were best for him. Because that's all who he really cared about these days—himself. He'd fired every single one of his employees at the casino including Caesar and officially closed down the casino. It had been a cruel thing to do, making people suddenly unemployed, but Kalmon could give anything but a fuck. He'd had his own flesh and blood fuck with his business so the last thing on his mind was anyone's feelings.

He'd also made sure to warn them of not telling a soul about what had happened at the casino with money being taken. What he wasn't trying to deal with was having *Hollywood Unlocked* or *The Shade Room* picking up the robbery story and letting the entire world know what had happened. His casino was still recovering from the 50 Cent drama, and he couldn't have another shit storm adding to the fire.

Whether Keon was totally behind the robbery, he truly didn't know. But what he did know was that Keon had a part to play in all the messed up shit happening to him and because of that, he couldn't trust him.

Jahana had called Keon after shooting Kalmon and now bags of money from Kalmon's casino had just mysteriously been dropped outside Keon's home. None of the things going on were truly making any sense to Kalmon, but the main culprit that kept popping up was Keon.

In order to stop himself from murdering his brother, Kalmon cut all contact with him. His numbers were blocked off his phone and he didn't want to see his face or talk to him. And as much as Kalmon missed his nephew, he couldn't bring himself to be around Athan when he had too much hatred for his father.

As for his family members and Azia, what Kalmon wanted was a break from them all. He couldn't be fake and act like he was okay when really and truly he didn't trust anyone right now. Not a single soul on this planet did he trust, and he just wanted to be left alone.

"Sir, we're taking off in five minutes."

Kalmon simply gave his flight attendant a stiff nod before reaching for his glass of cognac and downing it in one gulp.

A break was what he wanted and that was exactly what he was going to get. He was heading out the country, to his private villa in Monaco. A place where he could clear his head and be away from the problems in his life.

He'd left his attorney in charge of telling his mom and dad of his where-abouts as he didn't want them losing their shits thinking he was missing. He was going missing, yeah, but not actually going to be lost. He also knew Jahmai would be fine doing what he did best, managing their drug empire and as for the casino, that was staying closed until further notice. Reopening the casino would be something he would deal with when he returned.

He still had men looking for Jahana and they would keep him updated on their findings every single day. Kalmon just knew his heart wouldn't be at rest till he was able to wrap his hand around Jahana's throat and squeeze the life out of her.

"Relax, baby girl. Get some sleep, we've got a long ass flight," Kalmon informed Diamond who was anxiously staring at him through the door of her cage. She wanted to be let out so bad but Kalmon could do no such thing right now because they were about to take off in the jet.

"As soon as you wake up from your nap, I promise I'll let you out, D. Daddy promises."

Diamond started to ease up after his words, no longer looking at him so anxiously and deciding to relax.

"Good girl."

There was actually one person he trusted right now, and that was

Diamond. She was the only person he wanted to be around and he knew going away without her would have been difficult. So he made sure to bring her along. She was his baby at the end of the day. The only one he could trust 'cause she was the only person he was sure wouldn't stab him in the back.

* * *

YOU NEVER SAID anything about setting Keon Howard up.

What the fuck is that all about?

Send.

Caesar waited patiently for a response to come in and once it finally did, his face only twisted with annoyance.

Just relax. This is all part of the plan.

Unknown.

Caesar: *How is this a part of the plan when I don't have my damn money?*

Caesar: *You were supposed to steal the money, remove the trackers from the bands like I told you to and have my money ready.*

Caesar: *But you flipped the entire script and set Keon Howard up for the fall?*

Caesar: *That shit don't even make any damn sense.*

Caesar: *I want my money.*

When Caesar failed to get a quick response, he started feeling his body get hot.

Caesar: *Hello?*

Caesar: *You there?*

But still, no new text messages had come in, making Caesar quickly regret his entire role in this situation. All Caesar wanted was his money so he could leave town and somehow convince Nova to come along with him. And yeah, it was bad that he was willing to abandon his wife and unborn baby, but it was what it was. Even though it was a cruel way of thinking, Caesar just didn't care. What he wanted was his money so that he could start the life he so desperately wanted with Nova. He was hoping that once he had his cut from the casino money, he could prove to Nova that he was a millionaire and she would happily follow him out of New York. They would relocate to a brand new city far away from Kalmon Howard.

Now more than ever, Caesar was terrified. Even though Kalmon had fired all of his employees including him, Caesar had a hunch that Kalmon suspected him of being behind the robbery. And he didn't want to stay around to find out what happened to those that crossed him. In Caesar's mind, he had done a decent job in acting like he had no part to play in the robbery. And because he hadn't received his cut yet and couldn't flee the city, it made his story look more believable. But his worry wouldn't stop growing every single day. Kalmon Howard was a very smart man, and trying to fool him wasn't an easy task. Caesar didn't want to live his life in fear anymore, thinking that Kalmon had found out the truth and come to make him pay. He just needed to get what was his and leave the city before it was too late. But getting what was his was looking more unlikely now that the casino money was back in the casino. How was he supposed to be a millionaire now that the money was back in its rightful place? Caesar didn't care what had to be done, he just needed his money so he could disappear for good.

Chapter Twelve

H.E.R. really had a voice out of this world and her lyrics always knew how to resonate deeply in Nova's core.

I should've listened to my intuition
I've put myself in this position
It's all my fault, look in the mirror think what am I missin'?

As Nova walked through the busy New York streets with her AirPods plugged into her ears, the only person who remained embedded in her mind was Caesar. The one person who she'd told herself that she no longer cared about and wanted nothing to do with, was the only person she was thinking about.

He had a baby on the way with his wife but here she was being boo boo the fool and thinking about him. She still couldn't believe that he had lied to her for this long. And if it hadn't been for the casino night, she never would have even found out the truth. The worst part of all of this for Nova was the fact that even with all that he had done to her, she still loved him.

"It's good to see you, Nova. Back for your usual stuff already?" Kamiyah questioned her in a friendly tone.

"Not exactly," Nova replied with a chuckle. "I forgot to get my shampoo last time I was here and my hair dryer broke."

"Awww damn," Kamiyah voiced. "Well you know we've got whatever you need. You need help or you got it?"

"Oh I got it," Nova confirmed, beginning to walk down the long aisle leading to shampoos. "Thank you so much girl."

"You welcome, beautiful," Kamiyah told Nova, watching her walk away before looking down at her vibrating phone. "Hey, you don't mind if I take this quick phone call while you shop? It's my home girl and we haven't spoken in like for—"

Nova cut her off with a light laugh before stating, "No, go ahead love. Do your thing."

"Thank you so much!" Kamiyah exclaimed before quickly answering her phone, "Hey girl! What's up?"

Kamiyah was the shop assistant that Anaya had recently hired at the beauty supply. Not only was she a chocolate beauty but she was extremely friendly, something Nova greatly appreciated. This was only her second time meeting Kamiyah as Nova had only met her the last time she was here, wondering where Anaya was.

When Nova was at the section where shampoos were located, her eyes scanned the shelves looking for her favorite coconut hair wash. She quickly found it but once her eyes started wandering to the other hair washes, Nova started picking them up and examining them. That was the problem with Nova coming to the beauty supply store. She would swear she was here for one thing and end up leaving with over ten new products. That's why when she planned to visit, she always made sure that any plans she had with people were in the evening, hours after she was done with her shopping.

"...Key, you just need to tell me what the hell happened between you two..."

It was only five minutes into Nova shopping through the aisle she was on that she heard his heavenly voice on the aisle ahead.

"Fuck you mean don't worry? Nigga, you two are my brothers. I'm always gon' be worried…"

She could hear his footsteps walking through the aisle and by the sound of them, he was heading in the direction towards the back of the beauty supply.

"You know damn well I'm gonna find out one way or another. Just tell me."

Nova, being the curious individual that she was, decided to head towards the direction of his voice. She took quick strides towards the other side of the aisle until she saw the back door that he walked through.

Nova turned around momentarily to listen in on Kamiyah who had returned to her phone call.

"Yeah girl, sorry about that. My boss' fine ass son just walked in so I had to pause… yeah, that's the one… the things I would happily do to that man… you're nasty! I'm not sharing him…"

Nova decided to go to the brown door and gently pushed it open to walk through it. Getting to the other side and seeing stairs leading to a basement made Nova move fast. Once at the bottom of the stairs, she was greeted by a large stock room filled with various boxes that Nova knew contained beauty products. There were a vast amount of racks that held the boxes and as Nova examined the room, she realized she could no longer hear Jahmai talking on the phone. She took a few steps away from the stairs, interested in finding him until a sudden realization hit her.

What am I doing? She and Jahmai weren't even friends. Far from it. And here she was searching for him like she wasn't in his mother's private stock room. *Let me get my nosy ass out of here,* she mused, turning around with her basket in hand.

"Yo, where you going?"

But the sound of his deep voice stopped her right in her tracks, making her feel like a deer caught in headlights. She slowly twisted her body back around until she was able to see him leaning on the edge of the first rack in the room. Nova gazed into those mahogany pools of his and swore she could feel herself drowning in lust. It had to be a sin at how bad she wanted this man.

"Sorry I… I got lost," she lied, her nerves fluttering in her stomach.

"No you didn't," Jahmai said with a light chuckle. "Come here."

Nova looked behind her, thinking that maybe there was someone else behind her that he was talking to.

"It's only you and I in here, shorty," Jahmai reminded her as he watched her closely. "So you're the only one I'm talkin' to." He then pointed to the empty space in front of him. "Here. Now."

But as sexy as he sounded demanding her to come to him, Nova wasn't about to listen.

"I'm good standing right here."

"A'ight, I guess I'll just get you myself," he muttered in a tone loud enough for her to hear.

She observed him taking bold strides towards her and surprisingly, she didn't want to run. She wanted to see him get her himself. Once close to her, he climbed up to the step in front of her and grabbed her arm before gently leading her into the stock room.

Nova felt electricity flow through her body at his hold on her arm and as he led her towards the racks of products, her heart pounded away in her chest. When he eventually let her go, Jahmai pushed her against the rack and stayed standing in front of her.

"Why did you come down here, Nova?"

Nova's eyes were fixed on his, unable to break away from his captivating eyes. Hearing her name roll off his tongue was too alluring to her.

"I told you, I got lo—"

"Bullshit," he cut her off. "Why are you here?"

"I got curious," she admitted. "So I followed you. Is that a crime now?"

"Following men into unknown places… seems like you're trying to get yourself into trouble, Nova."

"Maybe I like the thrill," she commented with a light shrug.

"Oh really?" Jahmai's tongue seeped out his mouth and swiped across his lips. His eyes swept down her physique, admiring her long legs in her figure-hugging jeans and cleavage peeking out from her black v-neck tee, before his eyes swept back up to admire her gorgeous face. Unable to stop himself, Jahmai reached to hold onto her waist, caressing her body through her clothing.

"Maybe the thrill likes you too, Nova."

Nova's desire for this man was flickering to life with each passing second and the fact that he was touching her right now, had her picturing his hands on other parts of her body. But still within her crept a dying question.

"Why did you act like you didn't know me a few weeks ago?"

Jahmai gave her a hard stare before responding, "I didn't think explaining to my mom about how we met would have been a pleasant experience, so I acted like I didn't know you."

"You could have simply told her that we met at a party."

"Yeah, but that shit still would have felt awkward as fuck. We met at a party, yes, but at a party you were about to wild the fuck out in. So a nigga had to step in and stop you."

"I still don't like how cold you acted towards me, Jahmai."

Her saying his name made his dick harden even more in his pants, but he chose to ignore it for now.

"My apologies, shorty… all I could remember is the drama you were caught up in," he reminded her, using his free to reach up and run his fingers through her curls. "That nigga sure did a number on you, and it's a fuckin' shame 'cause you don't deserve that shit. At all. You deserve a man that's gonna take care of you the right way."

"And that man is you?"

"Nah," Jahmai said nonchalantly, removing his hands from her hair and her waist.

Nova's face scrunched up with bafflement.

"Huh? What do you mean?"

"Exactly what I just said," he affirmed, stepping away from her. "It ain't me."

"If it ain't you, then why you grabbing me and touching me like you want me?"

"'Cause I do want you," he admitted, shocking her. "Undeniably… but I'm not about to lead you on, Nova. I'm not looking for a relationship right now. That's just not the type of nigga I am."

"Who said I was looking for a relationship?"

He chuckled heartily before responding, "You say this now, but shit will change. It always does with you females."

"Females? You know that's another way niggas call women bitches," Nova informed him with a frown.

"My bad, Ms. Feminist. It always does with you women."

"I'm not looking for a relationship, Jahmai."

"You say this now…"

"I'm not."

"So what are you looking for?"

He gave her an intrigued look, waiting for her to answer his question. But instead of answering his question, she decided to walk over to him and reach for the back of his neck. She pulled him down nearer to her so that she could plant a kiss on his neck before licking his ear and beginning to suck on it. It was a simple act that made him want to cum in his pants.

"Nova... are you trying to get in trouble right now?"

"Maybe..." She kept licking and sucking on his earlobe, driving him crazy.

Jahmai wrapped his arms around her waist and pulled her nearer to him. He rested his face in her neck and deeply sniffed in her vanilla, fruity scent.

"You smell good," he complimented her sweetly.

"Yeah, I taste even better," she responded boldly, and that was enough to make Jahmai lose all composure.

"Uhhhh, Jahmai.... Ahhh, give it to me deeperrrrr, ahhh! Right... right there!"

"Right there, huh? That's your spot... shit. That's your fuckin' spot, huh?"

The back shots he was providing her with right now felt too good to be true. Too damn good.

"Yessss," Nova moaned as his powerful thrusts hit her deeper and deeper. "Right there baby."

"You take this dick so well, Nova," he groaned, reaching for her hair and pulling her hair back so she was forced to look up at him. "Too fuckin' well."

Good dick wasn't something that Nova came across often which was why when she did find it, she quickly became attached, one of the reasons why she had fallen for Caesar so quickly. And right now as

Jahmai's dick got well acquainted with her inner walls, Nova could feel herself getting attached.

"Open up your mouth for me, naughty Nova," he said moments later, making her do exactly what he wanted.

She had parted her lips for him and the next thing he did had her gushing like a fountain even more. He spat into her mouth before joining their lips together and kissing her. Pushing his tongue through her plump lips and mixing his salvia with their tongue battle. He was so damn nasty, and she really loved it.

If someone had told her yesterday that today was the day that she would be getting her back blown by Jahmai Howard, she would have never believed them. If someone had told her that she would be pressed up against a rack in his mother's stock room while he pounded into her from the back, she never would have believed that shit. But it was actually happening. They were actually having sex right now, and it was beyond anything Nova could have imagined. He was truly blessed with his size but also his stroke game. Nova was terrified because how was she supposed to now let this go?

It was something she knew she would want all the time; even as she had it now, diving in and out of her, she wanted it over and over again. That was terrifying to her.

Chapter Thirteen

Everything that had occurred with Kalmon was a nightmare to Keon. A nightmare that he wasn't sure he was ever going to be able to wake up from. This nightmare was showing no signs of disappearing.

Someone had tried to set him up with the casino robbery and the only suspect Keon could think of was Jahana. Somehow, from whatever hole she was hiding in, she had to be behind this whole fiasco. And because of the intuition he had, Keon knew he had to be the one to deliver Jahana to his brother. Delivering Jahana was the key to waking up from this nightmare and restoring the good relationship he had with his brother.

One thing that Keon didn't want to do was make things worse than they already were with Kalmon. So instead of reporting to their father and Jahmai about what had gone down with the casino money, Keon decided it was best he kept it between him and Kalmon. He made sure that Athena knew to not tell anyone about it. He'd also made sure to personally deliver the bags of money back to Kalmon at his casino. It was something he'd done the day after the incident, just before Kalmon had closed down the casino and fired everyone on sight.

At the end of the day, he and Kalmon were brothers and what had happened between them was going to be rectified. Because Keon was going to do whatever it took to get their relationship back on track.

"Daddy's gonna be gone a few days but I'll be back before you know it. Can you promise you'll be a big boy and take care of Mommy while I'm gone? Can you do that for me?"

Athan nodded enthusiastically at his father, making him smile with delight. Keon then pressed his forehead against Athan's small one, an act he did whenever he was about to depart from him. Then on that same forehead he planted a kiss.

"Athan, sweetheart, run along to your room while Daddy and I talk one last time before he goes."

Athan then nodded at his mother before doing as she asked and heading upstairs to his room.

"How long are you going to be gone for?" Athena asked him, seeing him place his last few items into his Nike duffel bag.

"For a while," Keon mumbled without looking at her.

The private investigator that Keon had on payroll had found a lead on Jahana in Beacon, a city on the outskirts of New York city. She had been spotted in a café ordering food but where she was staying was still unknown. The fact that she had been spotted was motivation enough for Keon to get out his city and go looking for her.

"I'm going to miss you, Key," Athena told him. "We're going to miss you."

Her mention of *we* made him look over at her to see her holding her stomach and gently caressing it. She was carrying the one thing he'd believed he wanted more than anything in the world. But now that he had it, he no longer wanted it with her.

Choosing to ignore what she'd said, he spoke up. "If there's an emergency, call me. But only if it's an emergency," he instructed her, zipping his bag.

"Okay," she meekly replied.

Keon knew she knew not to question him on where exactly he was going. He was going away on business and that's all she needed to worry about. Nothing else.

"Key…"

Hearing her call his name made his eyes scan over to hers once again.

"I really do love you and I'm sorry for what I did. I don't know what exactly it is you want me to do to show you how sorry I am, but I promise you I'll do whatever it is you want me to do. I just really want us to be good again, Key."

The genuine look in her eyes told him of her seriousness, but it did nothing to melt away the hatred he had for her. Every time he stared into her angelic eyes he could just feel his hate getting stronger. But it wasn't until he looked at her stomach that he managed to separate the hate he had for her and the love he had for his seed growing inside her.

Keon left his bedside and walked up to Athena and once in front of her, he placed a hand on her stomach and stroked it lovingly.

"Take care of my baby," he announced, dismissing every single thing she'd just uttered out her lips. "And like I said before, if there's an emergency, call me."

Athena just stared up at him and nodded, not bothering to challenge him on why he'd failed to respond to what she had told him.

Keon then went back to his bed, picked up his bag and headed downstairs to leave the house.

Once in his Bugatti, Keon started its engine with only one place in mind. He knew she was still at her bakery and wouldn't be finishing up till later, but he would wait for her undoubtedly. He had to see her before he left the city because honestly, he didn't know how long he would be gone for. He wasn't planning to come back to New York until he had Jahana tied up and blindfolded in the trunk of his car.

"He really hasn't hit you up? Man, what's wrong with that nigga? I gotta knock some sense into him my damn self, Zi. You see, that's why you shouldn't have friend zoned Nahmir; he's looking like the much better option."

Two hours later, her voice came seeping through her apartment and Keon sat up from the edge of her bed that he was laying on.

"Better not think he can just ghost on you and come back like nothing's happened. I'll fuck him up."

Getting into her apartment had been a piece of cake because after all, she had been the one to offer him a spare key. So he could come and go as he pleased.

"Yeah, yeah, but when he does come back, and trust me he will Zi, I'm gonna need you to stand your gro…"

Iman stopped talking when she noticed the shirtless man sitting on the edge of her bed.

"Zi? Let me…" Seeing his muscular physique and his chest of tattoos out on display made it hard for her to fully focus. "Let me call you back. Yeah girl. Bye."

She ended the call with Azia, sliding her phone into her back pocket and keeping her eyes fixed on Keon's.

"Keon, what are you… what are you doing here?"

He got up from her bed and took small strides towards her.

"How was your date, Iman?"

He hadn't forgotten about her telling him about her date last week and refusing to get out of it when he told her not to go. And he certainly had not forgotten her reminding him that she was not his girl.

"It wa… That's none of your business, Key."

Iman corrected herself mid-sentence, not wanting Keon to know about her date. Her date that she hadn't even attended because all she could think about was him. And knowing that she had made him jealous was actually something that gassed her.

Was she crazy for feeling that way?

"It sure as hell is my business, Iman," he announced with a tense glare, almost right in front of her. "When you know you're mine."

"No, I'm not," she mumbled, looking away from him, but it was short lived because he grabbed her chin making her look at him.

"You are mine, Iman. You've been mine and you will continue to be mine. If I have to remind you of that shit again, then I promise you there will be a problem between us. Now answer my question," he demanded. "How was your date?"

"There was no date," she revealed in a coy tone, feeling so turned on by how demanding he had gotten. "I never went."

"And why did you not go?" he asked, softly stroking her chin.

"Because, I didn't want to be on a date with another man."

Iman was lowkey surprised at how compliant she had become for him. Answering his questions and giving him much more than he had asked for. It was those seductive eyes of his for sure. Those eyes were making her wet in her panties at the sight of him.

"So why accept the date in the first place, MaMa, if you didn't want to go?"

"I wanted to see if I could forget about you."

"Wrong move," he voiced, before reaching for her throat and squeezing tight. "You can't and you won't forget about me, Iman. Especially not tonight when I'm deep inside your guts. You wanted to mess around and have a nigga pissed that you were going out with a corny ass nigga, making me lose my mind at the thought of him putting his hands on what belongs to me. So guess the fuck what? Tonight I'm fuckin' the shit outta you and making you realize that this ain't no damn joke. I'm getting deep inside you, Iman, and you're going to realize how deeply in love I am with you right before I make you cum. I'm done playing around; you're mine and that's that."

And after his speech, Keon leaned in closer to her lips and gave her a kiss that completely stole her breath away. He let go of her throat and moved his hands to her jeans, quickly unzipping them and sliding them down her body.

And Iman, being completely turned on and obedient to everything he had said, was now helping him take off his clothes.

The lovers frantically began stripping clothing from each other's bodies and it wasn't until they were both naked that they both landed on the center of Iman's double bed.

"Uhhh, Key... Key... I love you."

"I know you do, MaMa," he whispered, easing himself out of her. "And I love you."

He pushed his length back inside her and locked their lips in a passionate harmony.

He had been serious about no longer playing games with Iman. There was to be no more sleeping without him having her walls coated around his shaft. From here on out, they were to connect as lovers did and pleasure each other in ways words could not.

This moment right here, Keon never wanted to end. Her walls hugging his dick as he stroked inside her, refusing to let go, had his eyes welling up with tears.

Pussy so good, a nigga almost about to cry up in this bitch, he mused to himself, pressing back inside her cave. Only this time instead of leaving her snug passage, he stayed deep within her and slowly wound his hips in a circle.

"Keeeeeey!"

His motions made Iman cry out and become overwhelmed by the waves of pleasure he was providing. She dug her face into his neck, smelling his intoxicating aroma going inside her lungs, driving her even crazier.

"Key, mmh…. Shit, baby."

While he continued to wind his hips, his lips went to her neck where he began biting, licking and sucking on her warm skin. Giving her hickeys that he knew were definitely going to leave a red mark on her cocoa skin. And that's exactly what he wanted to make sure, so she knew exactly who she belonged to and never forgot that shit from here on out.

And after their climaxes had cum and gone, Iman lay under the covers while watching Keon get dressed and explain how he was going away on business and wasn't sure when he would be back. But he would keep her updated and call her whenever he could.

"I love you," he told her one last time and kissed her forehead.

Iman simply smiled and told him she loved him too. Then she watched him walk out the door, leaving her with her conflicted thoughts.

She loved him and he loved her, but was it enough? Was it enough despite how complicated their situation was? That was the question that Iman honestly did not know the answer to.

Chapter Fourteen

Nova couldn't get thoughts of this man out of her mind, which she didn't even understand herself because they hadn't known each other for long. How was she feeling this way about a man she barely knew? But he had known how to handle her body extremely well and provide her with a pleasure like no other.

Yeah what's good?

Jahmai.

It had been three days since he'd been inside her and now more than ever, Nova was experiencing withdrawal symptoms.

I've got a free evening and wanted to know if you'd like to come round? She typed back, butterflies flying in her stomach as she watched her message deliver.

His read receipt came shooting in minutes later.

Nah I'm busy.

Jahmai.

Her heart dropped at his reply.

Nova: *Okay.*

Nova: *No worries.*

Nova: *Another time maybe.*

Jahmai: *Shorty I don't want you getting your hopes up.*

Jahmai: *The sex was bomb but...*

Jahmai: *It was just sex.*

Jahmai: *I told you I'm not looking for a relationship.*

Jahmai: *Don't forget that.*

Nova: *Did I mention anything about a relationship?*

Jahmai: *You didn't but I know how this ends.*

Jahmai: *We keep fucking.*

Jahmai: *You catch feelings.*

Jahmai: *And then I'm forced to cut you off.*

Nova: *Let me save you the trouble of having to cut me off.*

Nova: *Asshole.*

She then clicked on his name icon, clicked info and went to the 'block this caller' section. And to make sure his number was added to her blocked numbers list, she headed to her phone settings, found the list and was glad to see his number.

What a fucking asshole.

She hated how entitled he was in calling all the shots and speaking nothing but his mind. And yeah, it had been her fault for letting him hit in the first place, but she didn't like how he was making her feel.

His constant mention of her catching feelings was only irritating her and because of that, she knew it was best she blocked him and forgot about his ass. As for his mother's beauty supply store, she would just have to find a new one. And as much as that burned her, because she loved Anaya's store, there was nothing she could do to change the reality of the situation. She didn't want to run into Jahmai, and that was bound to happen at Anaya's store.

Nova's eyes narrowed at her blocked numbers list and when her eyes stopped on a familiar number, her heart skipped a beat.

She had blocked his main number and the various numbers he'd tried to contact her through weeks ago. Surprisingly, he'd stopped using new numbers to get through to her and had left her alone. Nova lowkey wished that he would stay determined to get through to her because she wanted to see him try. And no matter how hard she tried to fight it, she knew she missed Caesar dearly.

Chapter Fifteen

I'm good. I just need some space. I don't trust anyone right now. Not even my own family. You're not my girl so just stop worrying about me and do you.

Kalmon.

Pow! Pow! Pow!

"Zi... you sure you're okay?"

Pow! Pow! Pow!

You're not my girl.

Those were the words that he had used in his text message five days ago.

Pow! Pow! Pow!

"ZiZi, sweetheart. Relax," her mother ordered, and she instantly obeyed, ceasing her punches to the heavy bag. "What's wrong?"

Azia took in quick breaths of air as she tried to return her breathing to a normal pace. She could feel her cheeks reddening with each second and she walked away from her mom to grab her water bottle on the nearby bench. She started to feel at ease once the fresh, cold taste of water ran down her throat, quenching her thirst.

"I'm fine, Mom," Azia spoke after drinking, but the brow that rose on her mother's radiant face told Azia that she was anything but convinced. "Mom, I'm fine."

"Are you sure?" Rivera questioned her daughter.

"I'm fine," Azia affirmed.

Rivera was still not convinced, but she chose to let it go. She knew that when Azia was ready to talk about what was bothering her, she would be here with open ears and comforting arms.

Once Azia finished up her boxing session with her mom, she helped her mom close up the gym. Rivera then gave her a lift home before kissing her goodbye once arriving.

Azia slammed her apartment door behind her and dropped her gym bag to the floor before heading to her shower.

For the past four days, rage had been building up inside Azia. Rage at the fact that Kalmon had the audacity to send her one lousy text message over a week after she had been bombarding him with calls and texts. It was only four days ago he had responded and to make matters worse, he had been rude as hell to her.

Stop worrying about me and do you.

Azia was honestly in disbelief at his sudden change of behavior towards her. He was treating her like he didn't care about her. Like she didn't mean shit to him, and she wasn't understanding. He had promised her months ago that he wouldn't break her heart and here he was, doing exactly that.

What had she done to deserve this treatment, she did not know. But one thing Azia wasn't about to do was sit on her ass, being depressed about Kalmon pushing her away. *Again.* He had pushed her away after his shooting and now something else had happened in his personal life and he was pushing her away again. She thought that they were supposed to be in this together... whatever they were doing together. She thought they were growing together as a couple and even though they had no official title on their situation, they sure as hell felt and moved like a couple.

But clearly she had thought wrong. It was dumb of her to assume that they were in a relationship. The way he was treating her now told her that she was dumb enough to believe that shit. He didn't even trust her enough to tell her what was going on with his life. Instead, he was pushing her to the side like she didn't matter to him. So she would simply do the same and push him to the side like he didn't matter to her. Because from this day onwards, he no longer mattered.

~ *The Next Evening* ~

"I'm surprised you finally decided to take me up on my offer."

"Why?" Azia shot him a curious gaze. "I agreed to doing drinks one day."

"Yeah you did, but now that we're actually doing it at my place, I'm surprised," Nahmir voiced, watching her lift her champagne flute to her lips.

"Good surprised or bad surprised?" Azia questioned him once sipping from her alcohol.

"A bit of both actually," Nahmir revealed, watching her carefully. "I'm lowkey worried your boyfriend might pop up at any time about to beat my ass or something."

Azia rolled her eyes at the fact that Kalmon had become their topic of discussion.

"He's not my boyfriend so you don't need to worry about him."

Nahmir's eyes widened at her response.

"Oh really? You sure about that?"

"Positive," she confirmed with a firm nod. "I'm single and no one's property."

"Hmm…"

"What?" Azia sensed he had something more to say by his lack of actual words.

"What if I'm tryna make you my property? In a non-objectifying way… Damn, I'm sorry. I shouldn't have asked that. If I offended yo—"

"It's fine," Azia cut him off with a light laugh. "I'm not offended. That was actually quite funny."

"That was my attempt at trying to be smooth," Nahmir said with a light sigh. "A wack ass attempt."

"No, it was cute," Azia told him. "It was real cute."

Nahmir's lips slowly curved into a smile as his eyes stayed fixed on hers.

"So if it was cute, does that mean I get an answer?"

Azia stayed quiet for a few seconds before deciding to answer his question.

"If you're trying to make me your property then I'd say you're in a great position to because you're now the only guy I'm talking to."

"Damn, what happened to ole boy who acted like I didn't exist that night at your apartment?"

"He's…" Azia let out a sigh as she paused, thinking about Kalmon but quickly pushing him out her thoughts. "He's no longer important."

"I see, I see… and I am?" Nahmir queried, curiosity growing in his irises.

"You've got me in your apartment with my favorite champagne despite the fact that we're not celebrating anything. I'd say you are pretty important."

"Yeah, but there's one thing you're wrong about, we are celebrating tonight."

"Oh, we are?" Azia observed him leaning forward with his champagne flute in hand. "What exactly are we celebrating?"

"Me being important," Nahmir stated, winking at her and lifting his flute towards her.

She too leaned forward and lifted her glass before pressing it against his so that they could toast.

The pair of them drank their remaining alcohol before placing their empty glasses on the black coffee table in front of them. It was the black table that divided them currently as Azia sat on the couch on the opposite side of Nahmir's.

"I sure as hell would love to kiss you right now, Azia... Can I?"

As soon as he'd mentioned them kissing, Azia felt her inner thighs burning up.

"You ca—"

Back, back-backin' it up
I'm the queen of talkin' shit, then I'm backin' it up
Back, back-backin' it up
Throw that money over here, nigga, that's what it's for

Azia's sentence was abruptly cut short by the interference of her ringing iPhone. She looked down at her bright screen sitting on the table ahead, noticing Iman's name as the caller ID.

It was currently 9 pm and Azia knew her best friend well enough to know that she only called this late if it was really important.

"I'm sorry," Azia began, reaching for her phone. "You don't mind if take this real quick do you? It's my best friend and her calling this late usually means it's an emergency."

She could see the glint of disappointment within his eyes but it vanished as quickly as his smile appeared.

"No problem. Feel free to head into my bedroom for some privacy," he informed her.

"Thank you so much, Nahmir."

Azia then rose up out her seat and pressed her green answer button.

"Iman? Is everything ok—"

"I'm in love with Keon even though I shouldn't be because he's in a relationship with my sister who is carrying his baby," she blurted out, making shock fill Azia's heart.

Azia quickly raced towards Nahmir's bedroom, entered and shut the door behind her.

"Iman... what... I'm..."

"I know, I know. Way too much info at once. I'm sorry, I should have warned you first but this has been making me feel guilty for days, Zi. I had to get it off my chest."

Azia took deep, slow breaths as she leaned against Nahmir's door, feeling overwhelmed with all that Iman had just revealed.

"... So you're in love with Keon," Azia said in a low tone, more to herself than Iman. "And he's with Athena who is pregnant with his child. Okay... right, got it."

"Remember the story I told you years ago of how I met Key first?"

"Yeah, I remember," Azia confirmed.

"And how I had feelings for him?"

"Those feelings never did go away, did they?" Azia questioned her, making Iman groan out.

"Nooooo. They didn't, Zi... they never went away." Iman's voice had become weak and from how quiet she had gotten, Azia just knew that she was crying.

"Iman, don't cry. Please don't cry. This isn't your fault."

"But it is, Zi!" she exclaimed, tears dropping out her eyes. "I slept with him and told him that I love him. I told him I love him when I know how my sister feels about him. I'm a homewrecker!"

"No you're not," Azia disagreed. "Don't say that."

"I am!"

"You're not. Please don't beat yourself up like this, Iman."

"How can I not beat myself up, Zi?" she asked Azia in a depressed tone. "I'm in love with my sister's man."

"You didn't just admit that you love him for no reason... the Iman I know wouldn't do that unless..."

"Unless he told me he loves me too," Iman finished off her sentence for her. "He did."

"So you're both to blame for this situation, Iman. 'Cause you both love each other."

"But Zi, we shouldn't love each other! He's not my man."

"Maybe he was supposed to be yours in the first place. Before Athena came along that day to the party. You were just too scared to step on your sister's toes," Azia reminded her of the event three years ago that had brought Iman, Athena and Keon together in the first place.

"Azia, Athena is pregnant," Iman boldly announced. "I can't compete with that. She won him. I need to let him go."

"Athena is pregnant, yes, but..." Azia's words faded off her lips as the reality of Iman's predicament truly hit her. "Shit. She's really pregnant?"

"Yes, Zi. She really is."

"... I don't even know what to say... this is shocking as hell."

"I know, I know."

"Like seriously, Iman... this is messy. This isn't like you."

Iman only sighed at the truth leaving her best friend's lips.

"It doesn't matter how much you were feeling him... Iman never would have done this shit. To her own sister?"

"Zi, it was a mistake," Iman tried to convince her. "A mistake that I just couldn't stop."

"So you only slept with him one time?"

Iman paused awkwardly for a moment before responding, "... One and a half."

"A half?"

"We didn't finish the first time."

"The first time?!" Azia shouted in disbelief. "Iman... you know how I feel about cheating so I'm just gonna keep it blunt with you as your girl. You need to end this before Athena finds out. Think about her and the child she's carrying right now. Think of Athan. They don't deserve this. They don't deserve to have their hearts broken by Keon but they most definitely do not deserve to have their hearts broken by you. End this now before it's too late."

Every single word Azia told her, Iman held on to. She didn't want to admit it at first, but Azia was 100% right. Athena and Athan didn't deserve this. Especially not Athena in the condition that she was in.

"You're right, Zi," Iman agreed with her wholeheartedly. "I need to end things with him. I can't go on like this."

"Exactly. This isn't healthy, Iman. You need to do what's right."

"I will," Iman promised, blinking back tears. "I will."

* * *

Nova's eyes fluttered open and she was greeted to the darkness of the room. She slowly turned her body out of her bedside to reach for her lamp which she switched on.

The second it was on was the exact same second she felt her body being pulled back into the bed. Her head twisted around and she was staring right into those captivating eyes of his.

He pulled her all the way into him and wrapped his arms tightly around her. No words came out his lips; instead, he branded their lips together in a hungry kiss, making Nova feel weak all over.

"I… love… you," he told her in between their kiss.

"I… know," she whispered to him before pulling her lips away from his. "But this can't happen again, Caesar. This was only for old time's sake, nothing more."

Caesar didn't respond to her words and pressed their lips back together. She claimed that this wasn't going to happen again, when they both knew she was lying. Caesar was back in her life and wasn't planning on going anywhere. He was here to stay.

Chapter Sixteen

Two Weeks Later

R unning through the bustling streets of New York on a weekend was something that Azia used to love doing. But with time she had become complacent and hardly bothered to come out her nest to jog. That was until a few weeks ago.

"Come on, Zi. You can do much better than that," Nahmir challenged her while jogging backwards, looking at her as she ran towards him.

Feeling determined, Azia boosted herself up and gave herself more momentum to accelerate, allowing her to speed straight past him.

"Ooooh, someone feeling a little more confident now?" he asked, catching up to her and running right alongside her.

"You bet," she revealed, grinning wide as they began to race. "I'm definitely going to beat you."

"Is that right?" he said in a teasing tone before suddenly grabbing her waist and pulling her back.

"Nooooooo! Get off me you cheater. Nahmir!" She laughed as he started kissing all over her face and down to her neck.

"Say the magic word and I'll let you go."

"Nahmir! Let me goooooo!" she protested, pretending like she wanted him to let her go when she wanted no such thing.

Nahmir continued to kiss up all on her and held her tighter.

"You really want me to let you go?" he whispered his question in her ear, making her look up at him.

For the past fourteen days, Nahmir had been the man easing the heartbreak she felt as a result of Kalmon pushing her away and dismissing her feelings. He was no Kalmon, but Nahmir was sweet and was there for her whenever she needed him to be.

They hadn't had sex since they had started talking again though. Azia wasn't looking for all that right now. What she wanted was good male company to keep her distracted enough from thinking about Kalmon.

But it was getting harder for her to fight the urge of not having sex with Nahmir. Especially when she was around him most late nights. And now as she gazed up into his brown irises, she could feel her body reacting to him. He was holding her pretty close to him too and only making her remember memories of him blowing her back out.

They'd had sex before in the past but Azia had taken it out the equation when she believed that things with Kalmon were getting more serious. She wasn't looking to have sex with anyone but Kalmon Howard. But fuck him. He hadn't tried to get in touch with her and apologize for the bullshit text messages he had sent to her, so he didn't matter.

Azia was done being stuck on him. He clearly didn't care about anyone but himself, so she would take his advice and stop worrying about him. It was a sudden act but he had been the one to suddenly text her and treat her like shit.

"No, I don't want you to let me go," Azia responded to Nahmir.

Nahmir's lips curled into a smile as he continued to stare down at her.

There was silence between them for a few seconds before Azia managed to escape out his hold and chuckle wickedly.

"'Cause I'm gonna get away from your ass and beat you!" she shouted as she began to run straight ahead down the westside highway they were running on.

"Oh we'll see about that!" he yelled back and began to chase after her.

Azia laughed while running far ahead, excited at their competitive spirt.

It was because of Nahmir that she had been motivated to get out and jog on Sunday mornings. He had hit her up one time and teased her about not wanting to crush her little spirit if they raced and he beat her. And of course, Azia being the determined woman that she was, she wasn't about to back down for anyone, which was why she decided to challenge him to a race.

Two Sundays had passed since their first race and now the pair went on regular jogs together. And to be quite honest, Azia was enjoying it quite a lot because she not only enjoyed getting back in shape, she enjoyed spending time with Nahmir. He was a very good distraction after all and she could feel peaceful knowing that she could spend time with him without being disturbed.

Azia was right about not being disturbed because the man watching her run across the westside highway through the tinted windows of his Bentley SUV was not going to disturb her.

"Let's go, Culhane," Kalmon instructed his driver.

"Yes sir."

His driver then moved out of the parking spot and headed to the main road.

Kalmon had returned from Monaco two nights ago. His trip to his private villa had proved to be helpful in clearing his head and giving him time to focus without being interrupted. For the first time in what felt like ages,

Kalmon actually felt happier. That was until what his eyes had just witnessed now. Happiness was the last thing he felt. And there was only one way he could get out of the foul mood he was in.

"Ahhhhh, Kalmo—"

"Don't moan my name," he snapped at her, and she slowly turned to look at him. "And don't look at me either," he ordered, grabbing her hair and forcing her to look ahead. "Just take… take this fuckin' dick."

Having sex with Lavena, the nurse who had been cleaning his wounds and providing his medication prior to him going to Monaco, wasn't exactly something that he had planned. But seeing Azia with the same nigga she had told him she was no longer going to have relations with had him pissed. Beyond pissed in fact.

What the hell was that nigga's name anyways? Raheem or Nathan something? He had completely forgotten because in his mind, that nigga wasn't important.

"Ughhhhhh, shit!"

The only way he could cool down was by giving Lavena backshots against his kitchen counter. He'd always thought she was a beauty from the second he laid eyes on her, and he also knew that she wanted him from the way she stared at him. And today his thoughts had been proven 100% right.

But even as he fucked her, there was only one woman on his mind. The woman who he had seen getting friendly and kissed up on by a nigga that she told him she was done with.

I leave for two weeks and she's getting friendly with some wack ass dude? I should fuck her up, and him.

And as much as Kalmon wanted to fuck them both up, he knew he was to blame for this entire situation. It was his fault that Azia had moved on because of the text he had sent her. His pride didn't want him to admit it, but he knew this was his fault. And because of his pride, he wasn't even about to storm over to her apartment and fuck some sense into her. He was just going to leave her be.

"I really enjoyed you... we should do this again."

Kalmon removed the condom from his dick and placed it in the nearby trashcan. Then his eyes fixed on Lavena's big brown eyes.

"Maybe," he stated nonchalantly, reaching for his boxers from the white tiled floor.

Having sex with Lavena had been decent. Not amazing but still decent, and for that reason alone, Kalmon knew he would never be inside her again.

"Well I'd really like to see yo—"

"Look Lavena," he interrupted her. "I've got shit to do right now."

"Oh," Lavena replied with a sad look. "So you want me to leave?"

"Sweetheart, you ain't gotta leave the building but you gotta get the fuck up out my crib."

Lavena gave him a look of dismay but said nothing more to him. She just began to get fully dressed.

"And don't bother showing up no more," he informed her on her way out.

Lavena looked at him one last time, seeing his eyes glued to his phone. It was evident not only by his words but his lack of focus on her that he just didn't care about her. *At least the dick was bomb,* she mused as she left his condo. *What a jerk though.*

Ding!

Food's been moving well.

Ding!

Everyone's well fed.

Jahmai.

Kalmon: *That's what's up.*

Jahmai: *How was Monaco?*

Kalmon: *Good.*

Kalmon: *Much needed.*

Jahmai was the only person out of his family members that he was speaking to on a regular. Kalmon could honestly say that Jahmai he could trust, because Jahmai hadn't given him a reason not to.

As for Nolita and Fontaine, Kalmon still hadn't bothered to call any of them. It was still just text messages he sent them. He didn't want to talk to his parents because he knew that they were going to harass him with questions about why he had fired all his employees. Kalmon was actually surprised that Keon hadn't told their parents what had happened between them. But Kalmon wasn't about to be the one to reveal all.

Jahmai: *You ready to tell me what happened between you and Key?*

Kalmon: *What's he said?*

Jahmai: *Nothing since I last saw him.*

Jahmai: *Ain't heard from him in a minute actually.*

Jahmai: *He mentioned something about going away.*

Jahmai: *I think he's left NYC.*

Kalmon: *Good.*

Kalmon: *His ass should stay gone.*

Jahmai: *Now come on Kal...*

Jahmai: *You know you don't mean that shit.*

Jahmai: *He's your brother and you're always going to love him. No* *matter what. You can stay angry with him as long as you like but it doesn't change the fact that he's your brother and he loves you. He would never betray you.*

Kalmon stared down at Jahmai's paragraph and sighed deeply. While in Monaco, all Kalmon could think about was Jahana calling out his brother's name and those bags of money being dumped on Keon's doorstep.

It still didn't make any sense to Kalmon. However, one thing he wasn't able to forget was the pained, teary look in Keon's eyes once Kalmon had uttered the words, *"You're dead to me."*

Looking back, Kalmon had only said that shit due to the heat of the moment. He hadn't actually meant that shit at all. But the heat of the moment had resulted in him saying some really hurtful shit to his brother, and he couldn't take it back.

Kalmon's main and only priority right now was Jahana. His goons still hadn't had any luck on her exact location, but they'd tracked her old phone to a motel in Beacon. A motel that she had dumped her phone in and fled from. She'd probably realized her mistake in keeping her old phone and failing to dump it before leaving Kalmon's city. So unfortunately, his goons currently had no new leads on her but were going to continue to search and sniff her out. Kalmon wouldn't be satisfied until he had her right in front of him, begging for mercy. He then took one last glance at Jahmai's message before locking off his iPhone's screen.

Jahmai looked down to see Kalmon's read receipt but no response to his recent message. However, Jahmai knew his cousin very well and knew that Kalmon was taking in what he had told him. Jahmai left his chat with Kalmon and scrolled through his messages, landing on a chat that he had forgotten to delete.

Nova: *Let me save you the trouble of having to cut me off.*

Nova: *Asshole.*

He grinned at the fact that she had blocked him. Her feistiness was one that undoubtedly intrigued him. It was one of the main reasons why he was attracted to her, among many other things.

He had meant what he said about not wanting a relationship, but that didn't mean he wasn't attracted to her. It didn't mean that she wasn't on his mind, because she was. Like 24/7. And at first it annoyed him because he believed that he was going to be able to forget her once being inside her, but his belief had been very wrong.

Because now she was all he thought about. He even dreamed about her. Dreaming about women? Jahmai barely did that shit, so for him to be doing it now and be dreaming of only her, he knew he had a situation on his hands. A situation that he wasn't sure how to get out of. Even speaking to his mother on the phone hours later didn't help him forget about Nova.

"You good, Mom? Sorry I ain't been to the store in a minute, been busy."

Jahmai had been busy indeed. He was Kalmon and Keon's distributor of their product, but he had his own property development company where he bought old houses, renovated them and sold them for much more than what he had originally purchased them for. His company also included him buying land, getting a new home built on it and selling it to make a profit. But just because he was busy didn't mean that Jahmai couldn't come check up on his mom at her store. The truth was, he had been avoiding the store because he had been avoiding Nova Harris.

"That's okay, baby. I'm good. Your dad and I would love to have you over for dinner soon though."

"Yeah, I'll be over as soon as I can," he promised. "You're both okay though?"

"Yeah, we're fine," his mother informed him calmly. "Just missing you is all, baby."

Jahmai chuckled lightly before replying, "I miss you both too."

Jahmai and his parents had an extremely tight-knitted relationship. He was their only child and meant everything to them. He was definitely more of a momma's boy though. Sure, he loved his father just as much and was grateful for the Howard name that his father had provided him. But if he was asked whether he was a momma's boy or not, he would definitely say he was one.

Jahmai's father, Makati Howard, was the younger brother of Fontaine Howard. Anaya Bennet had met Makati Howard when they were both teenagers in high school. By the time Anaya had turned twenty-one, they got married and once she was twenty-three, they'd had Jahmai. Twenty-nine years of marriage and Anaya and Makati Howard were still stronger than ever.

Fontaine Howard had started the Howard empire by himself at first, not wanting his baby brother to get involved at all. Fontaine preferred Makati being able to reap the benefits of their empire rather than actually getting his hands dirty. He wanted Makati's only focus to be on school. But once Makati finished college, he convinced his brother to let him help him and the two of them strengthened their drug empire.

Anaya had played a valuable part in helping the brothers too because she was the one that voiced her passion to start her own business to her husband. A black-owned hair and beauty supply store was something that she wanted because she didn't see enough black-owned beauty supplies. It didn't make sense to her how black people didn't dominate a market they provided so much revenue to and somehow, she was going to change that by dominating her own business.

Her idea was genius because the brothers could use her store to clean their money. And till this day, with Jahmai placed as the distributor, the hair and beauty supply store still proved to be efficient at cleaning money. But with how much weight The Howards moved through the streets, it definitely wasn't their only way.

"Baby, can I ask you a question?"

"Go ahead, Momma."

"What did you think of my best customer… Nova?"

And there it was. There was the million-dollar question Jahmai knew his mother had been dying to ask him for weeks now. It had finally arrived.

"She's cool," he simply stated.

"Just cool?"

"Ma…"

"What?" Anaya innocently asked. "I'm just curious to know what you think about her."

"So you ain't tryna play matchmaker?"

"No… but she's beautiful, right?"

Jahmai sighed lightly before responding, "Yeah, she is."

He could not deny Nova's beauty even if he tried to, and he couldn't deny how good it had felt to be inside her.

"She's breathtaking," he revealed in a low tone.

"So why can't I do a little matchmaking if you find her breathtaking?"

"Ma… you don't need to do all that. I told you when I'm ready to settle down it'll be on my own terms."

"I'm getting old, Jah… aren't you going to give your mommy some grandbabies?"

"Soon, Mom…I promise. Right now I'm focused on me and the business."

"And I get that but you don't need to be focused and lonely… You deserve to have someone to come home to every night, Jah. Someone to cuddle, someone to love."

"I love you, don't I?"

"You know what I mean, Jah," his mother voiced, making him chuckle because he knew exactly what she meant.

"I know, Momma. I'm just messing with you," he commented, smirking to himself. "But I hear you loud and clear. When the time is right, I promise you'll have your grandbabies."

"All three of them?"

"All three of them, Momma," he told her as a smile grew on his lips. "I promise."

Chapter Seventeen

"We're fifteen minutes away, miss."

"Thank you so much," Azia told her Uber driver before looking down at her flashing phone.

Iman: *He's not back from his business trip yet Zi.*

Iman: *And as long as it's taking... I don't want to tell him over the phone.*

Iman: *It needs to be a face to face thing.*

Azia: *Hmmm, okay, fair enough.*

Azia: *Just don't get weak at the sight of him.*

Azia: *Remember what you need to do.*

Iman: *I will.*

Iman: *I promise.*

Azia: *You told Nova yet?*

Iman: *No...*

Iman: *I was hoping to tell her at our next girl's night but we haven't done one in ages.*

Iman: *I miss those.*

Azia: *So do I.*

Azia: *Damn we need to do one soon.*

Azia: *We've just been all so busy.*

Iman: *Yeah, sadly.*

Iman: *But we have to have one real soon.*

Azia: *Definitely.*

Iman: *Have fun at Nahmir's!*

Azia: *Thanks girl, I will.*

Once arriving at Nahmir's apartment, Azia was welcomed into his home with a kiss and open arms. While they hugged, she admired his home over his broad shoulders. His apartment had such a manly feel to it, filled with dark colors such as navy, grays and blacks. But it suited him extremely well.

"I need to get you a key," he said, pecking her lips one last time.

"A key? Already? You sure you want me all up in your space like that? What if I'm a city girl here to rob all your shit?"

"You could rob me any day…" He paused to kiss her. "Anytime."

Azia laughed happily before walking out his arms to head to his living area.

"Don't be surprised if you come back one day and find all your furniture gone," she announced as she sat on his couch.

"Oh, I see you got jokes," Nahmir voiced, walking over to where she sat and joining her.

"Oh, you think I'm joking?" She gave him a serious look as she pointed at herself. Noticing the slight worry in his eyes made her burst into laughter. "I'm only messing with you."

He too broke into laughter before grabbing her hand.

"So tell me, how was your day, beautiful?"

Things between her and Nahmir were actually moving pretty fast these days. At first when they had reconciled, Azia told herself that they were just friends. But friends didn't kiss each other on the lips, go out on dates and flirt with one another.

They were definitely more than just friends and neither of them could deny it. And she was enjoying how things were maturing between them. It was like Kalmon had never existed.

Nahmir took the time to check up on her, make sure she was okay and even opened up to her about his personal life. He didn't push her away and that was why she felt so drawn to him. He was doing the one thing that Kalmon had failed to do: Keeping her close.

"You're really good at what you do," he complimented her minutes into their conversation.

"Thank you, Mir."

"No, seriously. You do so much for Howard Enterprises. Have you ever considered starting your own company?"

"My own company?" She gave him a wide-eyed stare. "That's crazy."

"No, it's genius because you would be running point on the entire thing," he informed her. "You would be the one calling all the shots without having to wait for someone to approve your ideas. You would be the one running the show."

Azia loved working for Howard Enterprises. And even though she hadn't landed her dream job making partner, she was still doing what she loved as marketing director. The thought of starting her own company had never crossed her mind because she liked working for a major company. But Nahmir had put a new thought into her head, one that she was strongly considering.

"You think I could just leave and start my own company?"

He nodded.

"One hundred percent. You're smart and you have connections with all the clients you've created big campaigns for. You've got good connections and so do I." He winked at her with a toothy grin.

"Oh you do, do you?"

"Yup," he confirmed. "I could help you take your company to a whole new level. Bigger than Howard Enterprises. Just think about it, baby."

And strangely enough, she was thinking about it. She was thinking about it a lot.

"You really believe I can build a successful company? All on my own?" she questioned him, slightly unsure of her worth and talent.

"Yes," he said, leaning in closer to her. "But you wouldn't be doing it all on your own. You'd have me right by your side."

He then moved closer to her until their lips were almost touching.

"Doing whatever you want me to do to please you," he whispered before pecking her lips.

Azia's eyes shut and her insides fired up with desire as he pecked her lips a couple more times, before beginning to kiss her deeply. Just when Azia placed her hand to the back of his neck, the sound of vibrating was heard. She pulled away from him to look over at his phone on his black coffee table. Nahmir followed her eyes and saw his vibrating device.

"You can get that if you want," Azia commented, noticing the annoyance grow in his eyes.

"Nah." He looked back over to her. "What I want is you."

He then drew back closer to her and joined their lips together. Her arms went to his shoulders pulling him close, and he pushed her back so she could lay down while his tongue explored her mouth.

* * *

JAHANA QUICKLY SHUT the door behind her with one hand pressed against her phone while the other carried her grocery bag.

"Ugh!" she groaned once hearing his voicemail, telling her to leave a message. "Nigga, what the fuck is wrong with you? I've been trying to get in touch with you for weeks now! Quit dodging my calls. I'm running out of money and I need you to send me some ASAP!" Taking a deep breath, she tried to ease her irritation and spoke up in a more calm voice. "Baby... please just call me back. I really miss you and just need to know when you're coming to join me. I told you I suspected I was being followed and you told me to move to Jersey and Nahmir, baby, I've done that, but you're still not here with me yet. Please, just call me..."

Her sentence faded and instead of saying anything else, she ended the call and chucked her phone onto the bed. Her eyes then scanned the small, dingy room and she blinked back tears as she contemplated about how life had gotten so bleak.

What was supposed to be a perfect plan had turned into anything but that. She was now a woman fearing every day for her life. Every day she feared that Kalmon would find her and it would be all over for her. Even though Nahmir had assured her that she was safe, she felt anything but.

Jahana placed her bag of groceries on the mahogany circle table before plopping her butt on her bed's edge.

Messing around with Nahmir was starting to look like a terrible mistake on her part. He was supposed to be here with her right now, by her side. After all she had done for him, he owed it to her. He owed it to her to be there for her, but that was the total opposite of what he was doing.

Dodging my calls? Who the hell does he actually think he is? He had no problems not dodging this pussy but now he's trying to act like he doesn't see me calling his ass? Maybe I should have shot his ass instead of Kalmon.

126

As quickly as that last thought came into her head, it quickly flew out because she knew she could never bring herself to harm Nahmir. She was falling in love with him for goodness sake. Harming him was impossible when he meant so much to her. She just wished he wasn't treating her so dirty right now.

Maybe he's just busy, girl. You know he's a busy man. Don't even trip. He'll hit you up and be with you soon. Just relax. He loves you, remember? He told you that himself.

Jahana nodded to herself before getting up from her bed and beginning to strip. The long ass afternoon she'd had meant that a shower was very much needed. And as much as she hated the water in this low budget motel, she had no choice.

Once completely naked, Jahana made her way to the bathroom and headed to the shower. She got in and began to wash her body while trying to soothe her worries away about Nahmir. Fifteen minutes later and she was out, now standing by the sink and staring at her reflection in the mirror.

Her reflection that told her she was sick of this shit. She just wanted to be living the life Nahmir had promised her they would be living together. *Be patient girl,* she told herself with a sure look. *Good things come to those who wait.*

Jahana gave herself one last look before heading out the bathroom back into her bedroom. But when she took a step into her bedroom, her heart stopped once she lay eyes on the man laying comfortably on her bedside with a gun on his chest.

She wanted to scream or better yet run, but that would have been dumb of her. The gun on his chest was loaded, she knew that. He would shoot her in an instant and not think twice about it, she also knew that.

"Jahana, Jahana, Jahana," he sang her name with a wicked grin. "Oh am I happy to see you, sweetheart."

Sweetheart. He had called her that knowing fully well she was anything

127

but his sweetheart. She had anything but a sweet heart after shooting his brother and almost leaving him for dead.

"If you're here to kill me then do it already," Jahana told him with a bold look, but deep down she was terrified.

"Oh I'm not here to kill you," he informed her, making her terror ease up slightly. "I'm here to take you to the man who's going to make you wish you were already dead."

Her terror intensified within her body, sending her mind into complete fright mode. Keon Howard had found her and was going to take her straight to the man she hoped she would never have to lay eyes on ever again. Nahmir had failed to protect her and now she was going to die.

Chapter Eighteen

One thing that Nova absolutely loved about her life was the fact that she was her own boss. An interior design company wasn't easy to run, especially when it was basically just her running the company. It wasn't easy, but it was fun. She loved being able to help new clients customize their new homes. Whether it was an entire home they needed designing or just a bedroom or even just a bathroom, Nova was their woman and there for them wholeheartedly.

Ding!

As she walked up to the building where her office sat on the fifth floor, Nova heard her phone go off and she pulled it out of her LV handbag only to stare blankly at it.

Can I see you tonight?

Caesar.

She didn't want him getting comfortable and thinking that they were back together or getting back together anytime soon. But at the same time, she wanted some dick. As a matter of fact, Nova was sure that she needed some.

Her mind refused to forget about the good dick down that Jahmai had given her weeks ago. And the only way she found herself forgetting about it, was by using Caesar as a distraction. Only from to time though because she didn't want him getting comfortable. They were not getting back together. This was just sex.

I'll let you know.

Send.

She then put her phone on do not disturb and headed through the building to make her way up to her office.

Nova rented an office space in this building where she met clients and did all of her paperwork. She also met up with her accountant here who helped her with bookkeeping and staying on top of her finances. Being self-employed wasn't easy but she was doing a pretty good job and of course, her accountant was a great help.

Once in the elevator, Nova watched the floor numbers go up on the small black screen above the doors. While watching, all she could think about was Caesar and how he was trying to prove to her just how much he loved her.

Every time they had sex, she could definitely feel him trying to persuade her of how sorry he was and how much he loved her. He could try and persuade her all he wanted though, it still didn't change the facts of the matter. He still had a wife and a kid on the way.

Yeah, you know this Nova, but here you are, still messing around with a married man. Like a dummy.

The elevator doors opened up and Nova walked ahead, ready to get into her office and start her day. Shaking all guilty thoughts about sleeping with a married man away. She quickly headed through the narrow corridor of closed offices.

The second she placed her key to the glass door, she was taken aback to find that the door was already open. It had been slightly left ajar and the force of her pushing against it with her key made it swing open farther.

She slowly pushed it all the way only for her to feel weak at the sight of the man standing over by her window wall.

He turned away from the view of the city to gaze at her standing in the doorway. Seeing her dressed in a light blue shirt dress with her legs out on display made his mind go cloudy with lust. She looked too damn good, especially with her hair up in a ponytail away from her glowing face. The ponytail he badly wanted to pull on as he entered her from behi—

"Excuse me, did you break into my office?"

Jahmai observed her placing her hands on her hips and her alluring eyes glowing with disapproval.

"I might have," he simply responded, pushing his hands into his pockets.

He was dressed in a khaki Adidas tracksuit with black Yeezy's gracing his feet. A casual fit nonetheless, but there was nothing casual about the things she was picturing doing to him, while looking at him.

"Nigga, leave," she ordered, pointing out her door. "I blocked your ass for a reason and that block exists in real life too. Buh-bye."

Nova waited for him to move towards the exit but when he stayed frozen in his stance with amusement dancing in his pupils, she could feel her irritation mounting.

"Jahmai, leave. Please."

"You keep ordering me around like you're the one in charge here, Nova," he announced. "I'm the one who broke in, remember?"

"Yes, I remember. You're committing a felony so when I call the cops on that ass, you'll be in handcuffs and you'll be humbled about being in charge." She pointed out the door once again. "Bye, Jahmai."

"How about I be the one to put you in handcuffs while you ride me?"

Oh my good Lord, Nova mused, feeling her entire body burn up rapidly.

Without her being able to control herself, the heat was only getting worse and worse.

"Jahmai... please, go."

"So you don't want to ride me, shorty?" he asked her, finally stepping away from her window and taking bold steps towards her.

With each step closer to her, Nova was sure her heart was beating closer to a damn heart attack.

"Y-You said you didn't want to lead me on," she reminded him, seeing how close he was getting and lowkey wanting to faint. "So why are you here?"

He was silent until he stood directly over her.

"'Cause I can't stop thinking about you, Nova." He cupped her butt with his palm, pulling her into him.

"I can't stop thinking about all the naughty things I want to do to you," he admitted, squeezing her ass tighter, resulting in her softly moaning. "All the naughty things I want you to do to me... my lil' naughty Nova."

A smile crept from her lips at him calling her his *naughty Nova*. It was funny, cute, yet sexy all at the same time, and she found herself smitten by it.

"If you want naughty Nova then you gotta stop treating me like I'm some delicate flower that's going to break any second," she told him confidently. "You said you don't want a relationship and I told you I never even mentioned that in the first place."

"I know, but after all that bull that nigga put you through, I just didn't want you expecting so much from me. As fucked up as this sounds, I don't cuff girls, I only fuck them."

"And how do you know I would even want to cuff you?" She gave him an arched brow. "You ain't even all that."

"Oh really? I ain't all that?"

"Yes reallyahhhhhhh! Jahmai! Ow!"

He chuckled before soothing the place he'd just spanked her on.

"When you talk all that shit, you get spanked, Nova. For being naughty."

"I thought you liked naughty Nova?" She straightened her body to press her lips to his neck, inhaling his seductive scent.

"I do, but when she gets too naughty, she gets spanked," he said before adding, "But I do like her... a lot. So much that I'm reconsidering the whole relationship thing."

Nova removed her lips off his skin to focus on looking up into his eyes. She saw nothing but honesty within them.

"I want you and I know you want me too," he announced while massaging her ass cheeks with both his hands. "I don't want to be the type of nigga that plays games with you, not like the last fool. The fact that I haven't been able to get you out of my head, speaks volumes to me Nova. And the thought of you being with someone else actually makes me want to shoot someone. And yeah, this is new for me, but I'm willing to try it, for you, shorty."

Nova actually couldn't believe all she was hearing right now. She thought he was here to play games with her but everything he was saying was the complete opposite of him playing games.

"You are?"

"Yes," he said, pecking her soft lips. "I am."

Usually when it came to two people getting to know each other and hoping to progress into something deep like a relationship, sex came later. But the pair had already put themselves in a position where their energies had been exchanged and he had explored the interior of the warm passage between her thighs. The sex had already come, but it didn't matter. Jahmai knew exactly what he wanted, and so did she. Having sex with Caesar again had been her little messed up way of trying to avoid how she felt about Jahmai. There was absolutely no avoiding it now.

"What you thinkin' 'bout?"

Jahmai could sense something was bothering her or at least something in her mind had caused her to drift off from their conversation momentarily because of the way her eyes had gone blank. He was starting to pick up on her little tells already.

"Just us," she admitted, vibrancy filling her eyes again. "I didn't expect all of this to be happening right now... but I'm happy it is."

"Good, 'cause this is just the beginning. I've missed you a lot and intend to show you just how much tonight after I take you out for dinner."

"Dinner sounds tempting," she replied, biting her lip at him. "But I'd rather just have my dessert right now."

"There you go, being naughty and shit," he remarked with a sexy smirk. "You want dessert right now?"

"I want dessert right now," she affirmed, looking up at him like she wanted to eat him up right this instant. "You've missed me, haven't you?"

"Fuck yeah I've missed your pretty as—"

All my life, been grindin' all my life
Sacrificed, hustled, paid the price
Want a slice, got to roll the dice
That's why, all my life, I been grindin' all my life

"Fuck," Jahmai cursed, letting go of Nova's butt to grab his phone from his pocket. "Hold on, sexy."

Nova watched as he brought out his phone, stared at the caller ID and quickly pressed the answer button.

"Nigga, where the hell have you been?"

He used his other hand that was still on her body to keep her close to him, not wanting her to think that just because he was on the phone she could leave his side.

Nova willingly pressed up against him and ran her nails through his bushy beard, stroking him affectionately. Their eyes stayed sealed on one another as he listened to his caller.

"Wait... what?"

The way his eyes grew large with shock had her slightly worried. His eyes had left hers too and he was now looking over her head.

"And where is she now?"

Nova silently continued to observe Jahmai on the phone, trying her hardest to listen in, but all she could hear was a male voice but could not actually make out anything he was saying.

"I'm on my way... yeah, I got you. I'll make sure he's with me. A'ight, no worries. Yeah I'ma call him right now. Okay, bye," he concluded before hanging up and gazing into Nova's eyes. "I gotta go, shorty."

She immediately pouted at his words.

"As much as I'd rather stay with you right now, I've got business to handle. Business that can't wait."

"You only just got here though," she reminded him. "You break into my office and now you're leaving without breaking my back out."

He chuckled at her before saying, "You're a lil' freak, you know that, right?"

She shot him a devilish smile.

"What can I say... being around you brings it out of me, Jahmai."

"I like that shit a lot though, so bring it out tonight when I come pick you up for our dinner," he informed her, pressing his forehead against hers.

"Okay."

Jahmai then pecked her forehead before branding their lips together and providing her with a sweet kiss. Once he pulled their lips apart, Nova was disappointed at the fact that it had to end already. He then pulled away from her, ready to leave.

"Unblock my number, shorty."

She smirked as she remembered what she had done, blocking his number.

"Okay," she agreed, watching him walk towards the exit and tapping on his phone's screen. He placed his phone to his ear once done tapping.

He turned around momentarily to give her one last smile and a wink before opening her door and leaving. Making Nova sigh with elation at all that had just went down with Jahmai.

"Yo, Kal..."

As his heavenly voice drifted down the corridor, Nova wished that tonight would come quick enough so she could enjoy her night with Jahmai.

Ding!

But her elation quickly disappeared once she reached into her handbag for her phone that was currently disturbing her wishes.

I really want to see you tonight Nova.

Caesar.

Now that things between she and Jahmai were progressing, she couldn't have herself in this complicated cycle with Caesar. Not when she genuinely liked Jahmai and didn't want to mess up what they were starting. Ending things with Caesar for good was something she needed to figure out how to do quickly. And in order for him to get the message, Nova knew she needed to end things in person. It would be the only way he would be able to look into her eyes and see that she was really done with him. It was over.

Nova: *I'm actually heading home now.*

Nova: *We need to talk.*

Caesar: *Okay great.*

Caesar: *What time should I come to your apartment?*

Caesar: *I can grab you some lunch if you'd like.*

Nova: *No lunch.*

Nova: *I'll hit you up when to come over.*

Caesar: *Alright.*

Caesar: *See you soon baby.*

Nova cringed at him calling her that but quickly reminded herself it would all be over soon. And the only person calling her baby would be Jahmai. The only man she truly wanted.

* * *

"ALRIGHT GUYS, so let me hear your new visual ideas for the new Mint Swim campaign Draya Michele wants us to handle. You know how much she loved our last one with her so we need to knock this one outta the park," Azia announced while standing in the center of her seating area.

She was currently having a meeting in her office with the creative team at Howard Enterprises to hear their concepts for bringing her idea to life. Draya Michele was the owner of Mint Swim, a bikini line for young women over the age of 18, and she loved the project that Azia had carried out for her last summer collection. Now she wanted to do another campaign with Azia and her team.

"So Azia, you said you wanted the model to be in a bikini but not in a stereotypical place, something out of the ordinary like a coffeehouse. So we came up with designs for the mod—"

Alissa, the lead designer, stopped talking upon the interruption of the door opening. Azia who had begun looking at the designs laid out on the table below her had failed to notice the person who had just stepped into her office.

"Alissa, why'd you sto—"

Azia found her words also coming to a halt as her eyes met his brown pools. She was breathless at the sight of him but at the very same time, flames of fury shot through her.

"I need the room," he announced, taking in all the faces sitting on sofas.

The creative team immediately began to move from their seats, obeying him without hesitation.

"No he doesn't," Azia retorted. "All of you stay right where you are."

The creative team gave each other looks of bafflement before sitting back down.

"Yes, I do," Kalmon voiced firmly, moving deeper into her office. "All of you get your shit and get the fuck out."

Once again the creative team got up from their seats, grabbing their things.

"Guys, ignore him. Sit do—"

"Azia, stop it," he cut her off. "I need to talk to you."

"No, you don't need to talk to me. You and I have nothing to talk about."

She actually couldn't believe that he had walked up in here like he hadn't done anything wrong. Like he hadn't ended them and pushed her away for good.

"I came to apologize and this is how you treat me?" He gave her a serious glare. "In front of everyone and I still don't get why you all are still fuckin' here. Leave!"

"Don't listen to hi—"

"Everyone get the fuck out before you no longer have jobs."

And upon him saying that, the creative team raced to get out of Azia's office without looking back. Eventually leaving Kalmon and Azia alone. Just how he needed it to be.

"Zi, I'm so—"

"Save it." She held her hand up and headed over to her desk. "I don't want to hear or care about anything you have to say. "

"Well you're going to hear and care about what I have to say today," he told her, sauntering to her table.

"Oh, the same way you cared about me when you sent me that text? Nigga, get out my damn office."

"I see that mouth of yours is still the damn same."

"Yeah, it is. And what?"

"Do you wanna have a smart ass mouth or have an intelligent conversation?"

Azia breathed out in frustration at the fact that Kalmon was in her office and talking to her like he was the boss here. Technically he was since his mother owned Howard Enterprises, but fuck that. He wasn't the boss of her.

"Zi, I'm sorry for that bullshit ass text… for pushing you away."

"Weeks later is when you want to say you're sorry? And you still think I care about you?"

Kalmon stopped at the front of her desk, watching her as she stood on the other side. All he could read within her eyes was pure rage. Nothing else.

"You no longer care about me? Is that the bullshit you're trying to tell me?"

"It's not bullshit," she fired back. "It's the truth."

"Oh, it's the truth huh?"

"Yes it's the truth! I no longer care about you Kalmon, the same way you no longer care about me."

"Azia, of course I fuckin' care about you."

"No the fuck you don't when you sent me that lousy text and abandoned me for weeks!" she yelled, feeling water fill her lids. "No you fuckin' don't. So quit lying!"

"Zi, I was going through some shit and I didn't want to take it all out on you. I needed to take some time to clear my head!"

"It's not an excuse! You treated me like shit, ghosted on me and have the audacity to waltz up in here like everything's good between us."

"I'm here to fix shit between us..." His words faded off his lips as he remembered what he had seen a few days ago. "But I can see your ass is not bothered about fixing us when you got that ugly ass nigga kissing all up on you on the highway."

Azia's brows snapped together and heat stained her cheeks at his words.

"How did you... you asshole! And why the fuck are you watching what I do?"

"This is my city, Azia. Did you forget that shit?"

"You're a fuckin' assho—"

"Call me an asshole one more time, I mothafuckin' dare you."

"And if I do? What are you gonna do, asshol—" She instantly stopped talking upon seeing him make his way around her desk towards her. Giving her déjà vu to a few months ago in his mother's office when he did the exact same thing.

"Kalmon, no," she protested, stepping away from him as he came towards her.

Her eyes swept up and down his clothed body, picturing his muscular body underneath. That body she had greatly missed.

"Stay away from me," she whispered, closing her eyes and she felt her back hit her wall. And the fact that his aroma was all she could smell right now told her that he was very close.

"How can I stay away from you when I'm in love with you, Azia Price?"

She felt like she was floating when she heard him question her, and she opened her eyes to take in the sight of him now towering over her.

"Y-You're not," she shakily answered him. "You don't."

"I love you."

Those three words that she had never heard from him before had finally seeped out of his lips. He had finally told her what she'd desired to hear from him weeks before the entire fiasco that had occurred between them.

"No you don't," she retorted.

"Yes. I. Do."

After each word he took a step closer to her and placed his hands on her waist.

"I love you, Azia Price."

She'd pictured this moment to be everything then. He would tell her that he loved her and she would say it back. One perfect happy moment. However, this moment right here was anything but happy.

"Quit saying that shit." She pushed his hands off her body. "When you don't mean it."

"Azia, what the fuck is wrong with you? I'm pouring my heart out to you right now and telling you I love you and here you are pushi…"

Fuck. Kalmon's realization at what Azia was doing hit him fast. Incredibly fast.

"Here I am what?" she asked him with satisfaction. "Finish what you were going to say. Here I am what?"

She really wasn't about to let him back in. He could see that from the emotionless look in her eyes. She looked dead behind the eyes. Even as he had admitted to her that he loved her, she failed to react.

What the hell have I done to her?

Pushing her away again for the second time had really fucked with her. He could see that clearly now, but one thing he wasn't going to do was let her go. Not now and not ever.

"I love you and I know you love me too."

Azia looked down to her light oak floor, fighting an internal battle with herself not to react to what he had just said.

"No matter how hard you keep tryna fight me away and convince yourself that you and I are done, Zi, I know you love me."

Why does he have to be right? She continued to stare down at the floor, trying her hardest to keep a blank face. And when her chin was lifted and her eyes were stuck on his, she refused to show him any emotion. In fact, the next words she uttered made Kalmon feel nothing but anguish.

"You don't value me, Kalmon."

"Of course I value you. What kind of question is that?"

"No, you don't value me, Kalmon," she repeated. "Because a person who values someone wouldn't ever put themselves in a position to lose the one they love."

Her words hit him straight in his core. And to make matters worse, he didn't have anything to say back to her. For the first time in ages, Kalmon had been silenced.

Fuck where your hoes at
Or where your Rolls at
Where your backbone, nigga, where your code at
Where your down since day one real bros at

The sound of his phone ringing broke the silence that developed between them. He gave her a depressed stare before reaching into his pants and pulling out his device.

His immediate plan was to silence it so he could somehow savor what little relationship he believed he still had with Azia. Until he noticed it was his cousin calling him.

"Jah? I'm kinda in the middle of..."

Azia watched his eyes drifting away from hers but they still held a deadly glare as he listened to his caller.

"I'm on my way."

He hung up the phone, placed his phone back in his pocket and grabbed hold of her face.

Azia was forced to look up into his eyes for a few seconds before she felt his lips crashing down to hers. Without her being able to stop herself, Azia yielded to his kiss. It had been ages since she had felt his lips on hers but now that she was feeling it, she never wanted to stop tasting him.

She willingly let his tongue explore the warm interior of her mouth and collide with her wet flesh. The more their lips synced, the more her body craved every single part of him. Then he let her go and ended their tongue battle.

"I fucked up. I know that shit but I promise you, baby. I'm gonna fix this. Stop messing around with that dumb ass nigga before you have to be a guest at his funeral. Diamond loves you and you're not allowed to stop being her mommy any time soon. And I love you. Don't forget that. "

Those were the last words he spoke before walking away from her and leaving her office. Leaving Azia with conflicted thoughts. On one hand, that man had been everything she'd wanted and more and on the other hand, she couldn't stand what he had done to her. She loved him even though she really didn't want to. And even though he was sure that he was going to fix things between them, she strongly disagreed. They were done.

Chapter Nineteen

This felt like a dream right now. The best dream that Kalmon had had all year. A dream that he was starting to lose faith in. But here it was.

"So you've really been looking for her all this time?"

"Yes. I told you I was gonna find her and bring her to you. Even with all the fucked up shit that's happened between us, I was never going to back out of my promise, Kal."

Kalmon kept quiet as he observed an unconscious Jahana who was currently tied up with tape on her mouth. She was really here right in front of him with nowhere to run. This was the best dream to ever come true for Kalmon.

"Wake her ass up," Kalmon ordered, and Keon nodded before getting in front of Jahana, removing the duct tape off her mouth and slapping her awake.

"Yo! Rise and shine, Jahana," he greeted her.

Jahana's eyes popped open at his second slap and she tried to move until she quickly realized where she was. She looked up at Keon who shot her a toothy grin before stepping back from her. Allowing Jahana to lay eyes on the one man that she dreaded having to see. Seeing him made her want to fall back asleep.

"You don't look happy to see me, Jahana," Kalmon announced, looking down at her.

Jahana kept silent but sweat now beaded her forehead.

"Why aren't you happy to see me, Jahana?"

She refused to speak up but a sudden blow landed on the center of her face, making her groan out. A blow that Keon had happily provided her with. He wasn't one to hit women at all, but Jahana had brought it out of him.

The punch dazed her for a few seconds and her face fell to the side. But when she felt her face being lifted and her eyes met his, tears shimmered in her eyes.

"Why aren't you happy to see me, Jahana?"

"Because of what I did."

"And what did you do?"

"I shot you, Kal but I'm sorry. I never should have hurt you! I'm sorry!" she begged.

Kalmon watched the tears running down her cheeks as he held her chin up. He placed a finger to her cheek, rubbing her tears away. Then he leaned in towards her left ear and whispered words that made her whole body go limp.

"Those tears won't save you today, sweetheart. I intend to chop up every single piece of you, bit by bit, making you feel every ounce of pain. Pain much worse than you had me in," he said before letting go of her chin.

"K-Kalmon, please. I'm so s-sorry. This wasn't my plan!" she yelled, alarm bells ringing in her head once she saw one of Kalmon's goons roll in a tray with a whole bunch of surgical equipment. And the fact that Kalmon was walking over to it was only making her more nervous.

"So why shoot him? And why try to frame me for that shit?" Keon asked her with his arms crossed, watching her carefully.

Jahana became silent once again. She was currently pressed up against a hard wall with nowhere to run or hide. The least she could do was try to somehow redeem herself from all the sins she'd committed. She told herself that she could never be the one to harm Nahmir, but now it was looking like she didn't have a choice.

"It wasn't my idea… it was Nahmir's."

"Nahmir who?" Jahmai piped up with a frown. "What's his last name?"

"Nahmir… Nahmir…" Jahana started pausing once coming to the realization that she had no idea what Nahmir's last name was. He had never told her.

Shit, I don't even know it.

"I don't know his last name, but he's the one that told me to shoot you Kalmon and frame Keon for it."

"And you listened to him?"

"Because I love…d him. I loved him," she said, trying to convince herself more than them that the love she had for this man was in the past. "He told me to do it so you two would have a rift between one another."

"Did he tell you why?"

Jahana shook her head to respond to Jahmai's question. By now, all three of the men were standing in front of her, focused in on what she was saying. Making her think that she had a fighting chance in saving her life.

"But he's clearly jealous of your empire. He told me you Howard men don't deserve the power you have and you need someone to knock you off your high horses."

"Wait, so let me get this shit straight." Keon begun stroking his smooth beard. "All that time you were begging me to help you get back with Kalmon, all that time you were messing around with a nigga that don't even fuck with him? With us? You really are one grimy ass bitch."

Kalmon couldn't help but chuckle after hearing Keon reveal what he had just been thinking about. It's like his brother had read his mind. All this time, Jahana had been getting dicked down by a guy that hated Kalmon while also trying to get back with Kalmon. She had to be on one serious type of crack that he didn't sell.

"He also wanted me to try and get back with Kalmon."

"See, now you're not making any damn sense," Jahmai snapped with a shake of his head.

"No, I am... his original plan was for me to get back in Kalmon's good books so he could somehow destroy your empire from the inside. He figured if I was back to being Kalmon's girl things would be easier in figuring out Kalmon's moves because I would be able to find out then tell him everything. But when that didn't work, he told me to shoot Kalmon. Once I met up with him, he told me to rip up the check Kalmon gave me and then told me to leave town."

"And you did all of this shit for him willingly because you loved him?" Kalmon shot her a skeptical look. "I gave you half a million fuckin' dollars and your dumb ass ripped that shit up instead of disappearing?"

"Yes," she said before adding, "and he promised me much more money than that."

"More than half a million?" Jahmai queried.

"Yes! Much more than that, and I believed him because the nigga is paid. He bought me more shit than you ever bought me, Kalmon. He actually loves me."

"If he loves you, he would be the one in that chair right now, not you," Kalmon told her. "He doesn't love you. He used you."

"No he didn't. He loves me!"

"Let me ask you a question, Jahana," Kalmon announced, taking bold strides towards her. "Have you ever been to the nigga's place? Been with him in the daytime when he wasn't fucking you? Do you even know where this so-called nigga works? Do you know if he was the one behind my casino getting robbed?"

Jahana listened carefully to each question Kalmon threw her way and felt her humiliation overcome her. They all knew the answer to every one of his questions. She didn't even have to say it.

"That's what I thought." He let out a hollow, callous laugh. "You let that nigga play you and think you could beat me when in the end, all he wanted was to drop your ass like he's done now."

"Kalmon, please don't kill m—"

"Remember what I told you about your tears not saving you today, Jahana? Well your screams won't save you either. So you can scream as loud as you want, sweetheart, no one's coming to save you while every part of your body is getting chopped up tonight."

Jahana wanted to scream but like he'd just told her, no one was coming to save her.

"Now I was about to do the lovely honors of cutting you piece by piece, but I no longer have time to waste on you," he explained with a wide smile. "I'll leave you to my man, Khaotic, who will take great care of you."

Jahana looked over at the man who had brought over the tray of surgical tools, taking a closer, deeper look at him this time. He had tattoos all over his ivory face, a bald head and a silver nose piercing. The sight of him made a chill run down her spine and it was at that moment, Jahana knew she couldn't go out like this.

"Kalmon please! Don't do this to me! I'm sorry! I'll do anything. Anything! I'll help you get Nahmir. That's who you want, right? I'll help you! I swear!"

"And how will you help us when that nigga refuses to answer your calls or texts? Matter fact, it's looking like he blocked your ass."

Jahana's face went white at Kalmon's revelation.

"Oh, you didn't think we knew all that did you?" Kalmon asked her. "See, while you were sleeping, Keon filled me in on all the activities of your phone. We already knew there was a Nahmir in your life before you admitted that shit to us. You were just confirming to us what we already knew and filling in the blanks. So thank you for that, Jahana. That was the one thing you could help us out on after all. But it changes nothing," he concluded before lifting the back of his shirt and pulling out his Glock.

Firing two shots into Jahana's chest, he made sure he shot in the exact same spot that she had shot him. The instant shots made her cry out in agony and shake in her seat.

"Close up those wounds so she doesn't bleed to death, drug her up and don't stop chopping till her head's left."

"Yes, boss," Khaotic replied before reaching for the adrenaline injection on the tray and walking over to her.

All three of the Howard men gave Jahana one last look, watching her scream and shake in pain from her gunshots but also fear for what was to happen to her. They then left the attic they were in and headed down-stairs to the main warehouse.

"I guess I owe you an apology, nigga," Kalmon voiced once the three men entered the empty room.

"You guess?" Keon chuckled.

"I mean... I might owe you a tiny one... nah, but for real bro, I'm sorry I didn't believe you about the shooting or even the casino robbery. I never should have told you that you were dead to me when I never meant that shit at all. I was just so damn angry, man."

"I know, bro. I know," Keon said in an understanding tone. "Just know I would never betray you. You're my brother and you mean the world to me. And yes, I admit at times I've not agreed with the way you make decisions behind my back, but I know deep down you make the decisions for the best interests of us. For our family. You've always been a protector and I've always admired that about you. Always."

Kalmon grinned at his brother before moving in close to hug him. The brothers hugged lovingly, making Jahmai smile and clap at their reconciliation.

"About time you babies got it together," Jahmai commented, pulling out his phone that had been on do not disturb for the past few hours.

Seeing a missed call from Nova made him smile harder. He would have to hit her up later though for their dinner date, 'cause he and his cousins had serious stuff to talk about now. He glanced at his gold Rolex to see it was almost 7:30 pm. Hopefully he would be able to get out of here in the next hour to go home and freshen up for the dinner date he had with Nova.

"But on a serious note, who the fuck is this dude Nahmir and how do we find him?" Jahmai asked firmly.

"I'm gonna do a database search and see what I find," Keon responded, reminding Kalmon of his younger brother's skill as a hacker. A skill he had missed seeing Key put to use.

"A'ight. He definitely must be the one behind the whole casino hit too," Jahmai voiced, making Kalmon nod in agreement.

"Yeah, 100%. The question is, was Caesar in on it too?" Kalmon queried.

"It was hella suspect how he didn't die too," Keon added.

While Jahana had been unconscious, that had given the men plenty of time to discuss the events leading up to today. From Kalmon's shooting, the robbery at the casino and Jahana's role in the situation. Now that Jahana had filled in the blanks, they knew she was merely a pawn in the plot against The Howards.

"But the money not ending up in his possession… if he was part of this shit, he would have got a cut," Kalmon explained. "But it still is suspect as fuck. I tried to not believe it 'cause of how much loyalty he's shown me, but fuck it. We gotta swipe his ass up and bring him here. If he's hiding something we'll get it out of him.

"Bet," Keon agreed, bringing out his phone. "I'ma run that database search up now and see what I find on Nahmir."

Ding!

The notification of a text came in from the only woman he wanted to be with right now.

You still coming round tonight?

Iman.

"We bringing in Caesar tonight?"

Keon: *Yeah, running a bit late though.*

"Yeah, let's swipe his ass around midnight. He'll be sleeping by then," Kalmon replied to Jahmai's query.

"I just need to know who the fuck this Nahmir guy is. Why's he trying us?"

"I don't know, but we gon' find out and once we do, it's curtains for his ass."

Keon: *But I'll be with you tonight, MaMa.*

Keon: *I promise.*

Iman: *Good, cause we really need to talk.*

Keon looked up from his phone and began to stare off into the distance. He really didn't like the text Iman had just sent him and it was making his mind circulate with worry.

You tryna go on a date again? He texted her back and remembered the night they'd shared before he'd gone away. The night he'd waited for her to come from her bakery, listened to her on the phone with Azia and fucked some sense back into her head.

"Key, you ready to bounce?"

Keon looked up at his cousin and nodded before replying, "Yeah, I…"

Ding!

Iman: *No.*

Iman: *We just need to talk.*

The more Keon thought about it, Nahmir was actually a name he had heard before.

Shit… wasn't that the nigga Iman mentioned while on the phone with Azia that night?

"Kal, shit… I think I know who Nahmir is."

Both Jahmai and Kalmon shot him a frosty look.

"Both of you stop looking at me like that, damn. I don't know him personally, but I think I know who does."

"Who?"

"Azia," Keon responded to Kalmon. "That's the girl you were messing around with, I swear."

"Nigga, he loves her ass," Jahmai testified, making Kalmon look his way and smirk.

"Yeah, why?" Kalmon questioned his brother.

"Now what I'm about to tell you both is gonna shock the hell out of you, but I'm just gonna go ahead and say it… Iman and I are in love with each other."

Jahmai was the first one to start laughing, thinking Keon was joking.

"Iman? As in Athena's older sister?" He laughed some more. "Yeah right, nigga."

But when Jahmai noticed that Keon's face was unmoved by his laughter, Jahmai realized his cousin's truth.

"Shit, Key... that's your girlfriend's sister."

"My ex-girlfriend who attempted to have an abortion behind by back."

Both Jahmai and Kalmon's eyes grew large with annoyance and shock.

"What the... Athena did what?"

Upon hearing Kalmon's question, Keon knew that he had a lot of things to fill his brothers in on. So he started at the beginning, from how he'd always had an attraction towards Iman but Athena had shown him the most attention. Then he spoke about how Iman had treated him at Kalmon's casino night and how he confronted her at her bakery. How Iman had accidentally told him all about Athena's abortion. How'd they fucked, didn't finish and Athan and Athena came over minutes later. How Athena told him how she never went through with the abortion and how Keon could no longer trust her. How Keon couldn't keep his feelings for Iman at bay, how'd they started sleeping together without actual sexual intercourse and how Keon had overheard Iman on the phone one night to Azia, talking about Kalmon ghosting on her and how friend zoning Nahmir had been a mistake. How Keon and Iman finally had sex together again that night and this time finished.

Once Keon was done talking, Kalmon could feel his pulse slamming in his neck and his muscles locked up with rage. There was no way that the nigga that Azia had been around all this time was Nahmir. And he had never known.

"Wait..."

A flashback of a conversation that Kalmon just remembered having with Azia flew into his head, making him realize something bad.

"So what's your reason for coming over at this time?"

"I wanted to see you."

"You wanted to see me?"

"Yeah."

"No, you just wanted to fuck. And so do I, so you're lucky."

"Oh, I'm the lucky one?"

"Yup," she concluded, and then ate off her fork while watching him.

"Five days without that smart ass mouth of yours. Yeah, I've definitely missed you."

"Nahmir and I used to mess around, but I officially ended things with him today."

He had heard the name *Nahmir* before! It was a name he had only heard one time and as soon as he'd heard it, he'd forgotten it because like he told her that night, that nigga wasn't important to him. Oh how wrong he had been. How fucking wrong he'd been!

Without saying a word, Kalmon raced out the warehouse, ignoring his brother and cousin shouting out to him and whipping out his phone to call Azia. He got sent straight to voicemail just as he hopped in his car and his jaw tightened.

"Azia, pick up the mothafuckin' phone! This ain't a damn joke! I ain't fuckin' playin' with you! Call me! Now! Baby, please… it's urgent. You're not safe and I need you with me now. Please baby."

He then hung up, chucked his phone to the empty passenger seat and started his car's engine to head to Azia's apartment. Now more than ever he needed her right by his side.

Chapter Twenty

"So I guess what I'm trying to say is…"

Originally, Nova told herself that coming over to see Caesar would be easy. She would have no issues laying it all out on the line with him, but here she was feeling nervous and not understanding why.

Maybe it was because deep down she knew, she still loved him. She loved all the times they had shared together before she'd found out about his wife and kid on the way. She'd loved how he had made her feel. Like she was the only woman in the world who truly mattered.

"Caesar, we need to end this. For good," she announced, watching him sitting across from her.

"Nova, you know how much I love you," he told her seriously. "How do you just expect me to let you go?"

"I expect you to let me go out of respect for your unborn child and your wife. Do what you should have done in the first place and let me go."

"I can't let go…"

Ding!

The sound of Caesar's phone going off sounded out, making Nova's eyes drift to the coffee table between them where his phone sat. Instead of Caesar reaching for it as she assumed he would, he ignored it.

"…of the woman that I lo—"

Ding!

"You should probably answer whoever's hitting you up," Nova advised.

"No, it's not importan—"

Ding!

"I think it is."

Caesar sighed deeply before obeying her and grabbing his phone. Nova observed him tapping on his phone screen for a few seconds before he locked his phone and pushed his phone back into his pocket.

"It's not important. You are."

His words said one thing whereas his face said another, because Nova noticed the stressed look he now had.

"Are you really about to end us when you know you're the best thing to happen to me?"

"Yes," she affirmed. "I am."

Caesar shot her a hurt look, but it didn't stop her from speaking.

"I was a fool to let you back in and I'd be an even bigger fool if I was to let you believe that you and I are going to be something. We had a good run but it's over, and I'd rather it stay that way. You don't have a choice on letting me go, Caesar. I'm telling you that you're letting me go, and that's that."

One of things Caesar had always loved about Nova was her determination. But right now, he hated it as he listened to her tell him how things were really done between them.

"So that's it then? That's how you really feel?"

"That's how I really feel," Nova stated as she got up from her couch.

"I've got plans tonight and I'd really appreciate it if you left my home now. Thank you."

Caesar took in the sight of her with her arms crossed, coming to the realization that things were really done with Nova. No matter how hard he wanted to be with her, he couldn't make her be with him. He wasn't that type of man and he wasn't about to start being that man now.

He then got up from his seat and slowly walked towards her front door. Only stopping once he reached it and turning around to face Nova who still stood by her couch with her arms crossed.

"I really am sorry for hurting you, Nova. That was never my intention when I lov—"

"That was never your intention but you did exactly that by lying to me about who you really are? Yeah okay, nigga." She chuckled lightly. "Get out my home, Caesar."

Feeling shot down by her remarks, Caesar reached for her doorknob and pulled open her door to leave.

Once the door slammed behind him, Nova breathed with relief and sat back down on her couch to relax. She looked over at the seat Caesar had been sitting on and a huge weight felt like it had been lifted off her shoulders and for that, she was glad. She could finally move on with her life without Caesar and focus on her new beginning with Jahmai.

She left her seat to reorganize her red satin pillows that graced her beige couch. It was only when she lifted the pillow that had been directly behind Caesar that she spotted his phone.

Damn, this must have slipped out his pocket. He'll come back and get it.

The thought of Caesar stepping back into her apartment, made her kiss her teeth with irritation.

I really hope he didn't leave this here on purpose, she mused as she pressed his home button to take a quick peek of his lock screen.

What she expected to see was a picture of his wife but what she actually saw was far from anything she was expecting. His phone had been on do not disturb so all his notifications had been silenced. However, now that she was looking at his screen she could see a string of notifications coming in from an unknown number.

Her forehead creased as she read the string of texts.

He will not find out, one read.

Just chill, another one read.

How many times do I need to you tell to…

She couldn't see the rest of the last message because it was too long so she decided to enter his phone. She knew his passcode because it was her birthday, something she had assumed he hadn't changed, and clearly she had assumed right. She entered his phone and headed straight to his messages where she was able to see it all.

He will not find out.

Just chill.

How many times do I need to tell you to relax?

Then she scrolled up to see what Caesar had been messaging the unknown number prior to the new messages that had come in.

Caesar: *Nahmir, where is my cut?*

"N-Nahmir?"

Nova's chest tightened as she read out loud the name of the man she knew to be Azia's friend.

Caesar: *I need to disappear.*

Caesar: *Fuck it all. I can't stay in this city no more.*

Caesar: *Something tells me Kalmon will figure out I had a role to play in all this.*

Caesar: *You said you were going to get the money back.*

Caesar: *Sorry hurry up and do that shit.*

Caesar: *Just give me my cut so I can get outta town with my girl.*

Unknown: *You mean your girl who wants nothing to do with you after finding out about your wife and kid?*

Caesar: *I'll be able to convince her to come away with me once I have my money.*

Caesar: *Just give me my mon—*

Knock! Knock!

"Nova!"

The sound of Caesar's voice and his loud knocking made her jump and drop his phone.

"Nova, I left my phone behind. Open up."

Nova remained frozen in her position, her heart now in her throat as she watched her front door.

"Nova?"

Knock! Knock!

There was no way she could open that door now that she had gone into his phone and seen what she had seen. She now knew that he and Nahmir had done something against Kalmon. What exactly they had done, she did not know yet.

Knock! Knock!

"Nova, you there?"

Nova quietly began moving around her apartment, heading to her bedroom to find her phone.

Knock! Knock!

"Nova, what the… open the door!"

His shouts only made her feel more uneasy, but she tried her hardest to stay focused on getting to her phone. Once she had it, she quickly headed to her contacts to find Jahmai's number and placed her phone to her ear once calling his number.

"Open up, Nova. I know you're in there. Let me get my phone! Nova!"

She could still hear Caesar from her bedroom and by the sound of things, his patience was growing very thin the more she stalled.

"Yo, it's Jahmai. I can't come to the phone right now…"

"No, Jahmai! Pick up! Please pick up!" she pleaded.

She then decided to call Azia but the same exact thing happened. The line went straight to Azia's voicemail.

"Why is no one picking up their damn pho—"

"Nova, don't make me break down this damn door! 'Cause I promise you I will."

Nova's heart pounded away as she realized that she was in the worst predicament ever. With no way to escape.

As easy as opening the door for him sounded, how could she bring herself to do it when she knew he was capable of betraying Kalmon? His own boss. And even Caesar would notice her change in behavior and upon seeing his phone, he would see that she had gone into his recent text messages and read all the new messages from Nahmir. His read receipts were on and the messages Nahmir had blown Caesar up with were now all read.

He would know she had read it and know that she knew his secret. Caesar had never hurt her before, but she wasn't sure what he would do to her now that she knew hints of his truth.

"That's it, Nova! I'm done playing with your ass. There's no way you've left the building 'cause I didn't see you come out. I'm coming in whether you like it or not!"

Chapter Twenty-One

I **man:** *He's officially back from his trip and coming to see me.*

Iman: *So I'm ending things with him tonight.*

Iman: *Wish me luck, Zi.*

Azia: *Good luck. You'll be fine.*

Azia: *Let me know how it goes.*

Iman: *Will do.*

Azia locked off her phone before bringing out her key to get into Nahmir's apartment.

Tomorrow was his birthday and even though he had been adamant on not wanting to do anything, Azia wanted to do something nice for him. After all, he had been such a great man in her life for the past few weeks, keeping her grounded and being great company. Nahmir cared about her and she even found herself opening up to him about her old situation with Kalmon. She had told him all about Kalmon pushing her away, not once but twice, and how she no longer wanted anything to do with him after how shitty he'd made her feel. Nahmir had listened to her when she needed a listening ear and not pushed her away… unlike *someone* else.

Azia sighed deeply as she thought about today's events. Kalmon coming to see her had caught her off guard and even admitting that he loved her had done that also. But what she wasn't about to do was fall victim to his charm.

She loved him but she didn't want to love him anymore. How could she love someone who constantly pushed her away and clearly didn't trust her? He didn't trust her enough to tell her what exactly had happened in his personal life for him to push her away. He'd only come to see her this afternoon making crazy demands like the crazy man that he was.

Azia walked through Nahmir's empty apartment and headed straight to his bedroom. She knew he was working late tonight because he had told her yesterday and so he was definitely not expecting the surprise she had in store for him.

Tonight was also the night she was going to reveal to him that she was finally going to listen to him and leave Howard Enterprises. She had already started drafting up her resignation letter and would be giving it to Nolita next week. As much as it was sad that she was leaving the best job she'd ever had in her life, Nahmir was right—she could start her own company. She was nervous but she knew Nahmir would be right by her side, helping her.

Azia placed her handbag on his bed, opened it up and pulled out her brand new lingerie lace set from Savage X Fenty.

She and Nahmir still hadn't had sex again since their last time together months ago. But now more than ever, all Azia wanted was for him to be inside her. Anything to somehow rid the feelings she had for Kalmon. So in a way, she was using Nahmir tonight, but oh well. Niggas did it all the time, so why couldn't she?

Azia got undressed out of her work clothes and took a shower. Then she dried up, creamed her body and got dressed in her lingerie.

She admired herself in Nahmir's wardrobe mirror, loving everything about how the hot pink lace complimented her golden skin. Her bra cupped her ample breasts lovingly, and she turned around to see her thong being eaten up by her plump cheeks.

She grinned at her reflection before deciding to oil her body one last time with jojoba oil. Once done, she took a seat on the edge of the bed with her phone in hand to see that the time was 7:30 pm.

She wasn't sure what time Nahmir would be back, but she would wait nonetheless. Azia got busy lighting Nahmir's bedroom with her favorite red raspberry scented candles. Once done, she got back on his bed and waited patiently. Waiting patiently resulted in Azia drifting off to sleep, only for her to wake up a few minutes later to the voice of Cardi B.

Back, back-backin' it up
I'm the queen of talkin' shit, then I'm backin' it up
Back, back-backin' it up
Throw that money over here, nigga, that's what it's for

She grabbed her phone and upon seeing Kalmon's name, she declined his call. Then she put her phone on do not disturb.

I'm not about to let him ruin my fun tonight. I'm surprising Nahmir and getting some dick. Period.

Azia started falling back to her slumber only to wake up an hour later when she heard someone enter Nahmir's apartment.

"Leave him. We can do this without you still being with him."

Hearing Nahmir's voice made her sit up and smile, glad he was back from work. By the sound of things, he was on the phone.

"But I'm sick of you being with him."

Azia reached for her phone only to see fifty-seven missed calls from Kalmon and a missed call from Nova. Out of habit, she took her phone off do not disturb and headed to her messages. *What the hell does his crazy ass want from me?* The fifty-seven missed calls from Kalmon made her roll her eyes with dismay. But it was the ten missed calls from Iman that made her mouth go dry.

"Athena, of course I love you. You know I do," she heard Nahmir say, making her face twist with confusion.

Did he just say Athena?

Azia's eyes landed on the texts from Iman.

Zi, please answer your damn phone!

Iman.

You're not safe with Nahmir.

Iman.

Key's told me about how he plotted with Jahana to cause problems between Key and Kalmon.

Iman.

Kalmon's been tryna get through to you and so have I.

Iman.

Where the hell are you, Zi? Please call me.

Iman.

What the... Azia could not believe her eyes nor her ears.

"You're carrying my kid for goodness sake, Athena. A kid I had to find out about from Kalmon's bitch who was on the phone with your sister... I overheard her talking to your sister and told you all about Keon messing around with her... you know they've been fucking and still, you haven't left his ass yet... Athena, your plan isn't working fast enough... you said we're going to destroy them, this was your plan and I went along with it out of the fact that I love you.... What the fuck is that supposed to mean? No, I'm not distracted. I was getting closer to that bitch and tryna sweeten her up so I could get more info on Kalmon, but she doesn't know shit about him. Her dumb ass doesn't even know he's the biggest drug dealer in NYC. So I'm simply spending time with her to make you jealous. And it worked, didn't it? You're jealous... quit lying,

166

Athena. Oh okay." He laughed. "No I haven't heard from Jahana since the last time she begged me to hit her up... you were the one that told me to get close to her, make her fall in love with me, have her shoot Kalmon and blame Key for it, and now you're blaming me for her downfall?... I'm not tryna argue with you baby, I'm just saying we need a new plan... yes... of course I still want this... I was the one that got Caesar to set his eyes on the casino, remember?... Yeah, we do need to get rid of him. He's weak and just won't work anymore... we've used him for what we want though... of course I do, baby.... you're the mother of my future child, Athena...I'll never stop loving yo—"

Back, back-backin' it u—

Azia quickly silenced her phone only now just remembering what she had done out of habit, taking her phone off do not disturb. Now she was realizing what a terrible mistake her habit had turned out to be. *Shit Azia. What the fuck is wrong with you?*

"...Hold on, Athena... I just heard some shit coming from my bedroom and I need to check it out. Some shit might have dropped but just hold, baby. Let me check it out."

Azia started hearing his footsteps move through his apartment. He was heading straight to his bedroom and she had nowhere to run and nowhere to hide.

From the desk of Miss Jenesequa

Wow. Wow. Wow. What a wow! Can I just say... all of my amazing readers who have constantly been harassing me for part two, I hope you liked this part! And if you did, you BETTER leave a review lol! And if you didn't, please also leave a review. I appreciate all reviews, good and bad. Let your girl know what you thought! As for where the next part is? Part three is on the way. Hang tight! But knowing you guys, you're all about to hound me down with messages of where part three is. LOL! I love you guys for that, I swear. I promise part three will be out soon! Thank you so much for all the love you've shown me on this book. It honestly warms my heart and keeps me motivated. You guys are honestly the best and the fact that you continue to show me so much love, truly means so much to me. I'll never stop loving you guys and appreciating you all so VERY much.

Please head over to my official website where you'll be able to see the visuals of Kalmon and Azia including the rest of the gang: www. missjenesequa.com. My website also includes **ALL** the visuals from my previous works, so don't hesitate to go check it out! On my website you can also find out more about me and see my entire catalog. If you liked this book, then you'll definitely love my other completed series so feel free to check them out! And make sure you join my private readers group on Facebook to stay in touch with me and my upcoming releases: www. facebook.com/groups/missjensreaders.

Trust me when I say my readers group is LIT! If you're not a part of it then trust me…

You. Are. Missing. Out!

To all my ladies in my readers group, you all are the best and thank you for understanding me and loving #PettyJen just the way she is!

I'll be posting sneak peeks from the finale in my readers group, so make sure you're a part of it! Thank you so much for reading! My readers mean the world to me and I'm never going to stop letting you guys know that.

Love From,
Jen xo

Miss Jenesequa is a best-selling African American Romance & Urban Fiction novelist. Her best-known works are 'Bad For My Thug', which debuted at #1 on the Amazon Women's Fiction Bestseller list, 'Loving My Miami Boss', 'He's A Savage But He Loves Me Like No Other' and 'Sex Ain't Better Than Love' which have all debuted top 5 on Amazon Bestseller lists.

Born and raised in London, UK where she always dreamed of becoming successful at anything she put her mind to. In 2013, she began writing full length novels and decided to publish some of her work online through Wattpad. The more she continued to notice how much people were enjoying her work, the more she continued to deliver. Royalty via Wattpad found Jenesequa and brought her on as a published author in 2015. Her novels are known for their powerful, convincing storylines and of course filled with drama, sex and passion. And they are definitely not for the faint-hearted. If you're eager and excited to read stories that are unique to any you've read before, then she's your woman.

Stay Connected

Miss Jenesequa's Reading Room

Feel free to connect personally with Miss Jenesequa at:
www.missjenesequa.com

Thank you so much for reading! Don't forget to leave a review on Amazon. I'd love to know what you thought about my novel. ♥

ALSO BY MISS JENESEQUA

Sex Ain't Better Than Love 1 & 2

Down For My Baller 1 & 2

Bad For My Thug 1 & 2 & 3

Addicted To My Thug 1 & 2 & 3

The Thug & The Kingpin's Daughter 1 & 2

Loving My Miami Boss 1 & 2 & 3

Crazy Over You: The Love Of A Carter Boss 1 & 2

Giving All My Love To A Brooklyn Street King 1 & 2

He's A Savage But He Loves Me Like No Other 1 & 2 & 3

Bad For My Gangsta: A Complete Novel

The Purest Love for The Coldest Thug 1 & 2 & 3

The Purest Love for The Coldest Thug: A Williams Christmas Novella

My Hood King Gave Me A Love Like No Other 1 & 2 & 3

My Bad Boy Gave Me A Love Like No Other: A Dallas Love Novella

The Thug That Secured Her Heart

Royalty Publishing House is now accepting manuscripts from aspiring or experienced urban romance authors!

WHAT MAY PLACE YOU ABOVE THE REST:

Heroes who are the ultimate book bae: strong-willed, maybe a little rough around the edges but willing to risk it all for the woman he loves.

Heroines who are the ultimate match: the girl next door type, not perfect - has her faults but is still a decent person. One who is willing to risk it all for the man she loves.

The rest is up to you! Just be creative, think out of the box, keep it sexy and intriguing!

If you'd like to join the Royal family, send us the first 15K words (60 pages) of your completed manuscript to submissions@royaltypublishing-house.com

LIKE OUR PAGE!

Be sure to <u>LIKE</u> our Royalty Publishing House page on Facebook!

CPSIA information can be obtained
at www.ICGtesting.com
Printed in the USA
LVHW091820290819
629406LV00006B/855/P

9 781686 437328